My Kind of Girl

An Enemies to Lovers Lesbian Romance

Reba Bale

MY KIND OF GIRL

© 2024 by Reba Bale

MY KIND OF GIRL

AI training and development of machine learning language models.

Cover by Aila Glass Designs

CONTENTS

About This Book

How many chances will it take before they give into their feelings?

Ava

My mother is getting tired of waiting around for a grand-child, so now she's on a matchmaking mission. But I'm not ready to settle down just yet, especially with someone my mother picks out for me. Except there's something about Kathy...could it be that she's my kind of girl after all?

Kathy

I didn't realize a dinner invitation from a fan was really a fix-up with her beautiful daughter. Too bad Ava is de-termined to hate me on sight, because we keep running into each other in the most unexpected places. Despite miscommunication and dating disasters, dislike is starting to feel a lot like love. But can I trust her to let me be my quirky self?

Sometimes the path to happily ever after is a little rocky...

"My Kind of Girl" is an enemies to lovers second chance lesbian romance. Expect steamy scenes, a wacky best friend, a meddling mom, and a little bit of luck leading to a sweet happily ever after.

This book is part of the *Second Chances Lesbian Romance* series. Each WLW book in the series is a standalone sapphic romance featuring two strong women finding love the second time around.

Join Reba Bale's Newsletter

Want a free book? Join my weekly newsletter and you'll receive a fun subscriber gift. I promise I will only email you when there are new releases, free books, or special sales you'll want to see.

Visit my newsletter sign-up page at https://books.rebab ale.com/lesbianromance to join today.

CHAPTER ONE -- BEAUTY AND THE SNEAK ATTACK

"**A**re you sure you're really a lesbian?"

I peeled the cucumbers off my eyelids and carefully turned to look at my mother on the next table. She was usually quiet during our monthly Mother/Daughter Beauty Day, so the question came out of the blue.

"Yeah Mom, I came out to you when I was fifteen years old, remember?"

Mom nodded, the movement making her own cucumbers slide from her eyes. She carefully put them back in place.

"It's just that you're thirty now and you don't seem to be able to find a woman to settle down with. I was just wondering if maybe you're bisexual or something? Have you thought about trying to date guys?"

I took a deep breath, inhaling the eucalyptus scent that came from a diffuser in the corner.

"I have literally never been attracted to a male," I said adamantly. "And thirty is not that old."

"It is if you're ever going to give me some grandchildren. You've only got a few more good reproductive years left. Your clock should be ticking."

The esthetician who was rubbing cream on my face snickered quietly.

"Well that's the great thing about dating women, Mom. If I'm too old and decrepit to be inseminated when I'm ready to have a family, hopefully my wife will be young enough to take one for the team."

"Ugh, you make it sound so...unromantic," Mom grumbled.

"You're the one hot for grandchildren, not me. I don't even know if I want kids."

My mother gasped like she was in pain. "Of course you want kids. Can't you at least do it for me?"

"Mom, I'm not going to have a child for the sake of your vanity."

She sighed deeply.

"Well I guess we'll have to write you out of the will and leave all of our money to a horse sanctuary in Wisconsin or something."

It was a frequent threat, but a toothless one. My mother hated Wisconsin, like every good Chicagoan did. Plus, as the only daughter of parents who owned hotels all over the world, my position in the will was pretty secure. At least I thought it was. My father would never let her go through on her threats.

"What about one of those menage relationships?" my mother asked, just as the salon owner came into the room to check on us. I felt the tips of my ears turn red, as my mother continued, "I've read about polyamorous relationships in romance books, they sound very fulfilling."

"I don't want a menage relationship, or any type of polyamorous relationship. I'm just waiting for the right girl to come along."

When my mother made an impatient sound, I continued, "I want what you and Dad have. A forever love. Hopefully after I'm forty because I'm way too young to be tied down right now."

Truthfully, I had been thinking lately that it might be good to settle down, but I figured I'd give myself a few years before I started looking for that special someone.

"Make up your mind Ava. Last week you told me you were old enough and mature enough to be moved up into the C-Suite at the company, now you tell me you're too young to get married and have kids. Which one is it?"

"Can't both things be true?" I asked.

"No." My mother's voice was firm. "I told your father I would veto any more promotions for you until you can prove that you're emotionally stable enough to be in something for the long haul."

"What are you even talking about right now, Mom?" I demanded. "I've been working for the company since I was fourteen years old. How is that not in it for the long haul?"

My family owned a very successful luxury hotel chain. Like my mother before me, I'd started cleaning rooms as a teenager, working in almost every job we had before earning a position in management. My parents weren't ones to let nepotism get in the way of hard work.

I must have frowned because the esthetician made a soft sound of disapproval as she massaged the wrinkles out of my forehead and the furrow between my eyebrows.

"What was wrong with Jane?" my mother asked, changing tactics.

"Which one was Jane again?" I asked, purposely blocking her out like I had with every loser my mother had tried to fix me up with.

"The Phillips girl. The one with the unfortunate overbite."

A picture flashed in my mind of a very masculine woman with no body fat, no boobs, and the same haircut as my mother's driver had. Not that there was anything wrong with any of that, but it wasn't what I found attractive. I liked my women to be...well, womanly. I loved manicures and make-up and girlie shit and while I didn't need a partner to be as femme as I was, I at least needed her to be a little bit femme.

So sue me, I liked what I liked.

"I didn't find her attractive," I said mildly.

"And Suzie Holloway?" Mom asked, "What was wrong with her?"

She was secretly dating a woman her parents would never approve of because the girlfriend wasn't from a wealthy family. Suzie swore me to secrecy.

"I wasn't attracted to her," I said.

"Well exactly what kind of girl are you attracted to?" my mother asked in exasperation.

"I'll known when I see her."

CHAPTER TWO -- AMBUSHED

"What are you wearing to dinner tonight?"

I pulled the phone away from my ear, verified that I was actually talking to my mother, then then asked, "What? Why does it matter?"

I had Sunday dinner with my parents every week. If it was up to my mother I'd also join them for church, but this was the compromise we'd reached several years ago.

Mom had never – not once – been concerned about what I was wearing to come over for dinner. As soon as my parents came home from church, they'd both pull on their athleisure and lounge around for the rest of the day. They both dressed up in suits and heels (my mom anyway) and they'd told me a million times that once church was done, it was their time to dress comfortably.

She was up to something.

"What's going on, Mom?" I asked in my sternest voice.

"Nothing." Her voice rose at the end, a sure sign she was lying. It was also a useful tell when you played poker with her.

"Mom!"

I let the silence hang for a full minute. She broke first.

"Okay, I might have invited someone over to dinner to meet you. She's such a sweet girl and she'd be perfect for you."

I rolled my eyes so hard I was surprised I didn't strain a muscle.

"Mom."

"Look Ava, if you're not going to even try to do something about your chronically single status, then I will. I want that grandchild."

Her voice turned stubborn, and I knew it was hopeless to even try to argue with her. Whoever this mystery woman was, I was going to be stuck having dinner with her.

"Who is she?" I asked. I wondered if the woman was even a lesbian. Mom had fixed me up twice with women she thought "looked like a lesbian" but turned out to be straight.

"It's no one you know," she said. "Wear a dress."

"I will not wear a dress."

"Well, at least wear something clean and unwrinkled then," Mom bargained.

"Fine."

A few hours later I arrived at my parents' house on the Gold Coast. I'd purposely worn faded jeans, running shoes, and a plain pink knit top. It was a tiny step up from my usual dress, but not much. I'd pulled my dark curly hair back into a high, messy ponytail, and my face was completely free of makeup.

When I let myself into their townhouse Mom gave me a disapproving look, then mumbled, "You could have at least left your hair down. You have such pretty hair."

"It bugs me when it's on my neck," I rejoined.

"Hi Sweet Pea," my father folded me into a big hug. "It's good to see you."

He said that every Sunday, but I knew he meant it. Even though we worked in the same building, I didn't see either of my parents very often at work. That would change when I got my next promotion. If I got my next promotion...

"Are you ready for this?" Dad said softly. "You want a drink?"

"Yeah, I'll have a shot of whiskey on the rocks, please."

When my father gave it to me, I knocked it back in one gulp, even though it was expensive sipping whiskey. Without a word, he gave me another, but I intended to savor this one. I just needed to take the edge off my nerves.

It wasn't the first time my mother had blindsided me with a fix-up, although usually they happened when we were out to lunch together, and some eligible woman just "happened" to run into us. This was the first time she'd tried a fix-up on her home territory. Clearly she was upping her matchmaking game.

The doorbell rang and Mom hurried to answer it, while Dad put a hand on my shoulder as if he was afraid that I was a flight risk. He wasn't wrong.

I looked up as Mom led a woman through the doorway to where we were waiting in the living room. My breath caught in my throat for a second. Whoever this woman was, she was stunning.

She had dark brown hair and huge brown eyes that stood out against the paleness of her face. She was wearing a dress that hugged her delicious curves, the fabric stretching over her breasts and hips before ending mid-thigh, revealing strong legs and an adorable pair of chunky heels.

She'd be exactly the kind of woman I'd go for, if she wasn't in cahoots with my mother. Maybe it was immature of me, but there was no way I wanted to have anything to do with a woman my mother wanted to fix me up with. Something had to be wrong with her.

"Good afternoon," she said, her greeting encompassing me and my father.

I ignored the thumping in my chest and the overwhelming desire to grab her hand and drag her home with me where

I could feast on those curves for hours. Instead I affected a chilly expression.

"Hi, I'm Ava."

Something flashed in her eyes at my tone, but when she spoke again, her expression was carefully neutral.

"Hi, I'm Katherine, but my friends call me Kathy."

"Nice to meet you, Katherine," I replied with deliberate intent.

Her eyes widened slightly at the insult, then her expression shuttered, her eyes becoming dim. I felt like an asshole knowing that I'd put that expression on her face, but I was in self-protection mode here.

My mother gave me a sharp look before turning to put her arm around Katherine.

"Well, now that you girls have met, shall we eat?"

CHAPTER THREE—A PAINFUL DINNER

"You two have a lot in common, you know."

My mother's gaze bounced between me and Katherine. *Kathy.* We were seated across from each other at the dining room table, and every once in a while she'd give me an uncomfortable look. It made me wonder what she knew about this dinner before accepting the invitation.

"Like what?" I asked.

"Well, to start with, you're both lesbians."

I couldn't help but roll my eyes at that one. When I glanced at Kathy, one corner of her mouth quirked up. It was kind of adorable.

"You're both thirty."

"Actually Mrs. Morganstein, I'm thirty-two," Kathy corrected.

"Much too old for me," I rejoined. I was rewarded with another quirk of Kathy's lips. For some reason, I couldn't stop looking at them. They just looked so soft and pink.

"You both love animals," Mom continued undeterred. "Oh, and you both have a head for business."

"How exactly do you know my mom?" I asked Kathy.

"We go to the same coffee shop."

Silence fell around the table as we all picked at our food. Well, except my father. He kept on eating like everything was perfectly normal. His ability to be oblivious to my mother's shenanigans was impressive.

"Do you work at the coffee shop?" I asked Kathy, mostly to be polite, but partly because I was curious about her despite my best efforts. She didn't look like she was a barista, but then again, what did I know?

"No, but I *do* my work there," she said, poking at an asparagus spear on her plate.

When she didn't elaborate I asked, "So what kind of work do you do?"

Kathy gave me a look, one that told me she'd decided that I wasn't worth her time. Not that I blamed her, I'd been kind of rude to her ever since she arrived. Yet for some reason, it bothered me that I'd hurt her feelings.

"Kathy is a writer, isn't that exciting?" Mom gushed, breaking our little stare down. "She writes, um, what did you call it, dear?"

"Sapphic paranormal rom coms."

"What now?" My father spoke up for the first time the entire meal.

Kathy gave him a friendly smile. "I write romantic comedies about supernatural creatures like shape shifters, vampires, and witches, with sapphic characters. Mostly lesbians, but some who are bi or trans or non-binary."

My father looked sorry that he'd asked. He'd always been cool about my coming out as a lesbian, but he felt pretty strongly about people who he felt "can't make up their minds" about their sexual orientation like bisexuals or non-binary folks. He struggled to understand the nuances of gender and sexual orientation.

Before he said something that would embarrass me or make poor Kathy even more uncomfortable, I interjected.

"Do you write books, or do you do those serial things?"

"Books," Kathy said. "I'm published on all the major on-line bookstores."

Well, that was impressive. I knew not everyone could get a book published.

"She was a best seller with her last release," Mom rushed to add. "The top of the Amazon charts, I saw it myself."

Kathy blushed and it was super cute. "Only in the lesbian fiction category."

"Still, I was so proud of you when I looked at your book and saw that orange best seller banner."

"This meal was delicious Mrs. Morganstein," Kathy said, clearly wanting to change the subject. "Thank you for inviting me and welcoming me into your home."

"I'm glad you enjoyed it," my mother said warmly. "We'll let you girls clear the table and we'll meet you in the living room for dessert."

My parents hustled out of the room, leaving Kathy and me sitting there in the dining room staring after them.

"That was really subtle," I finally said.

Kathy nodded. "Yeah, I guess in retrospect I should have considered that your mom was trying to fix me up with someone when she invited me for dinner."

"You didn't know?" I asked.

"No. She never mentioned you, although she did ask me if I had a girlfriend and what kind of woman I like," Kathy explained. "We've been talking on and off in the coffee shop and got to know each other a bit. She seemed really fascinated with me being an author too. I thought maybe she was a little lonely so when she invited me I figured she just wanted to talk about my writing. Plus she went on and on about her famous pot roast so I figured what the hell, it would be nice to have a home cooked meal. Of course I texted my friend the address and pictures of the house in case I wound up locked in your mother's basement or something."

"Turns out she had something way worse than the basement planned for you," I said in a dramatic voice.

"What?"

"Foisting off her unmarried daughter."

CHAPTER FOUR – DISHES AND TINGLES

"What kind of work do you do?" Kathy asked as we worked together to clear the dining room table.

I leaned closer to her to grab a serving dish and couldn't help but notice that she smelled really good. Like orange blossoms. I wondered if it was her hair or some kind of cologne.

"I work at my family's company," I said. "I'm a marketing manager."

"What's the company?" she asked, following me into the kitchen with an armful of dishes.

"M&M Luxury Hotels. We own several hotel chains around the world."

Her eyes widened. "I guess that explains why your parents' kitchen is larger than my entire apartment."

I watched her carefully, looking for any sign of subterfuge. Over the years, I'd noticed that people generally fell into two groups: those who knew exactly how wealthy my family was and wanted to capitalize on it, and those who pretended to not know who we were so they could capitalize on it. It was pretty unusual to meet someone who had no idea who we were, but I couldn't see an iota of deceit on Kathy's face.

"You didn't know who my mother was when she invited you to dinner?" I clarified.

"No, like I said before, I thought she was just a lonely old lady. Honestly, I figured it would be just me and her eating pot roast and talking to her cats. When the map app on my phone brought me here I thought for sure I'd written down the wrong address. I didn't expect there to be a husband here, let alone a daughter."

"Surely you've seen our family on social media or on the local society pages?" I pressed.

Kathy shrugged. "I'm not a fan of social media, and I didn't even know they still had society pages. I only rarely watch TV."

"If you don't watch TV, what do you do for fun?" I asked.

"I spend a lot of time in my writing cave. I go days, sometimes weeks, without talking to a real human other than by text or email. If it wasn't for the grocery delivery services, I'd probably starve to death hunched over my laptop. Even between books, I don't have a lot of interest in social media."

"But you do have social media?" I asked.

"Oh sure, my author persona does. I pay someone to manage all that for me. I don't have any personal social media though, other than the fact that I belong to a couple of writers groups on discord."

"Wow."

I couldn't say why, but I believed her, as unlikely as her story was. Kathy seemed incredibly down to Earth.

"Those can't go in the dishwasher," I said, pointing at my mother's crystal wine glasses. "I'll wash them in the sink."

Kathy pushed the dishwasher closed, then hunted around for a dish towel. "I'll dry."

I filled the sink half full with soapy water and made quick work of washing the four glasses that my mother only brought out for special occasions. As I washed, I'd hand the glass to Kathy who would dry it and set it on the counter.

"This is the last one," I said, handing her the fourth glass.

Our fingers grazed over the sink, and I heard a sharp intake of breath before Kathy practically snatched the glass away from me and dried it. Suddenly the air between us felt heated and I was aware of everything about her: the way she smelled, the heat of her skin, the way her dress hugged her curves. I looked her over hungrily and when my eyes finally made it up to her face, she was watching me.

She looked a little bit confused. I reached a hand out to her, then let it drop. Kathy turned to face me and when she licked her lips, I couldn't help the soft groan that moved up my throat.

"You know Kathy, you're a very attractive woman."

"I'm sensing a 'but' there," she said wryly.

"I'm not really looking to date right now, especially with someone my mother picked out. No offense."

"No offense taken."

She stepped back and gave me an arch look. "Just so you know, I'm not looking to date either. But I wouldn't have minded getting laid."

My mouth dropped open but before I could say anything Kathy gave me a little wave.

"I've got to get back to my writing cave. Nice to meet you, Ava."

CHAPTER FIVE – AN UNEXPECTED REUNION

*S*ix months later...

"This is exactly what I needed today!"

I rolled my head to the side to give my friend Marcella a smile.

"Yeah, it's been way too long since we came to the beach."

Living in Chicago, there were only a few months out of the year when it was warm enough to go to the stretch of beach along Lake Michigan. Today was the first day of the year when the temperature was expected to go past ninety, so Marcella and I couldn't resist heading on down to Oak Street Beach.

It was a Friday afternoon, and Marcella and I weren't the only two people who'd left work early to enjoy the sunshine. The beach wasn't super crowded, but there were definitely more people milling around than I expected.

"I'm going to dip my feet in the water," Marcella said, getting up from her blanket.

"Are you kidding me? You know that water is going to be frigid still!" I reminded her.

It would be another month before the water was tolerable enough to go in, but the sand was warm and the skies were clear, so I was perfectly content.

"Just my feet," she said. "I can't go to the beach without touching the water, you know that."

I waved her off with my insulated water bottle. "Have fun."

I leaned back on my elbows, staring out at the water as Marcella walked slowly down the beach. My skin prickled right before I heard someone say, "Ava Morganstein? Is that you?"

A goddess appeared in front of me, her shape blocking out the sun. I had an impression of lush curves and strong thick thighs. Breasts that strained against the thin fabric of her pink one-piece bathing suit. I studied her face, trying to remember how I knew her.

Holy shit. It was Kathy, the woman my mother had tried to fix me up with last winter. The one I could have probably could have fucked if I hadn't been such a jerk to her.

"Kathy, right?" I asked, rolling to my feet.

"I'm surprised you remember."

Her tone was frosty, making me wonder why she'd stopped to talk to me. Maybe she just wanted me to see her banging curves in that suit, giving me a taste of what I missed.

The truth was, I'd thought of her several times over the past few months. After she'd made that announcement about just wanting to get laid, she'd flounced out of the kitchen, said goodbye to my parents, and left before I even knew what was happening. My mother had assumed that it was my fault Kathy left and was so irritated with me about it that I left a few minutes after Kathy to avoid her wrath.

"I remember all the women that my mother suckers into ambush dates with me," I said lightly.

It wasn't true. I'd never given any of them a single thought other than Kathy. For some reason, she stuck with me. Maybe because I was actually attracted to her. Or maybe because my big mouth and rude behavior had ruined my opportunity to have sex with her.

Kathy's eyes slid down my body, and without conscious thought I sucked in my gut and subtly arched my back to put my breasts at their best angle. I was wearing a two piece suit that consisted of high-waisted red bottoms and a red and white bikini top that tied behind my neck. It wasn't skimpy or anything – it covered all the important parts – but under Kathy's perusal I suddenly felt naked.

One corner of her mouth quirked up as she noticed my hardened nipples pressing against my bikini top.

"It doesn't feel cold out here," she joked, and I felt annoyed at her calling attention to my body's very normal response to being checked out by an attractive woman.

Then I noticed that I wasn't the only one affected.

"Seems like your body feels cold too," I said, waving at her breasts.

To her credit, a flush of red creeped up her face.

"Well, I saw you here and just wanted to say hello. See you around, Ava."

She turned to leave, and my hand shot forward, catching her wrist.

"Wait."

CHAPTER SIX — FUN IN THE SUN

"Wait."

Kathy looked down at where I held onto her wrist, then looked over her shoulder at me. With her sunglasses on, I couldn't tell what she was thinking. I couldn't tell if she felt the tingles of electricity where my fingers wrapped around her wrist the way I did. It made my breath hitch in my throat.

"Did you want something, Ava?" she asked coolly.

I deserved it. I was rude to her at my mother's house, yet she'd been the one to initiate contact today. That had to mean something.

"Are you, um, here alone today?" I asked lamely.

"Yeah, I just got here." I noticed the large tote bag on her shoulder.

"Why don't you join me and my friend?"

She turned to face me but for some reason I continued to hold onto her wrist. I liked the feeling of her skin against mine.

"I'm fine alone, thanks."

"We have snacks," I added in a sing song voice.

I could practically feel her rolling her eyes behind her sunglasses. I leaned in closer, bringing my mouth close to her ear. This close, I could smell her shampoo. It reminded me of peaches.

"We have contraband wine," I whispered.

She shivered. "You snuck in wine?"

"Please," I scoffed, pulling away from her even though I was dying to stay close. "What kind of a Chicagoan would I be if I didn't sneak alcohol into places where it's not served?"

She smirked. "Okay, since you have wine, I guess I could join you. If your...friend won't mind?"

We both glanced over at Marcella who was waving at me from a distance. Even this far away I knew she was dying to know who I was talking to. My best friend was nosy as hell.

"She's a platonic friend," I said firmly.

"I wasn't asking," she rejoined.

We both knew she was lying.

"Pull up a towel," I said, pointing to where Marcella and I had stretched two giant beach towels side by side on the sand.

Kathy set down her bag, pulling out a rolled up towel that she set up about two feet away from mine. Gracefully she lowered herself to the ground, then dug into her bag again, this time pulling out some sunscreen. I tried not to watch as she rubbed the creamy liquid over her pale skin.

"Need any help?" I asked just as Marcella reached us.

"My my, who do we have here?" Marcella asked with a big smile.

Kathy looked up from slathering on sunscreen.

"Hi, I'm Kathy. I'm kind of friends with Ava's mother."

"But not Ava?" Marcella asked, looking between us with amusement.

"No," Kathy said shortly.

Marcella rolled her lips in to keep from laughing. "Well I'm Marcella and I'd love to be your friend, baby."

Did I mention that my friend was the biggest flirt in Chicago? Men, women, nonbinary people, she didn't care. She flirted with them all.

I expected Kathy to rebuff her, but instead she giggled. The sound was sweet and light, and it set my teeth on edge.

My friend dropped her ass on the bottom portion of Kathy's towel and started chattering away. Kathy seemed to take to her right away, talking and laughing as Marcella grilled her about her relationship status, her job, and her hobbies and interests. Within ten or fifteen minutes, Marcella had gotten to know Kathy better than I had during the two hours that I spent with her at my mother's house all those months ago.

I couldn't say why it bothered me, but it definitely did.

"Now how did you meet my friend Ava here?" Marcella asked.

"Her mother invited me for dinner after we got talking in a coffee shop. I thought she was just some lonely old lady, but instead it was an elaborate plan to fix me up."

"With Ava?" Marcella said, like it was the most ridiculous thing she'd ever heard.

"I know, right?"

I ground my teeth at Kathy's joking reply.

"Do you want some wine?" I interrupted, thrusting one of the insulated water bottles towards Kathy. "No one's drank out of this one yet."

"Thanks," she said, unscrewing the cap and taking a healthy swig. "Yum."

My gaze fixed on her upper lip where moisture gathered.

"You got a little..." I gestured at her face.

"Here," Marcella said, stretching out a hand. "I'll get that for you."

Chapter Seven — Jockeying for Position

"She knows how to wipe her own lip," I said harshly, surprising myself with my vehemence.

For some reason, the idea of Marcella touching Kathy was making me see red, which was weird because I wasn't a jealous person. Oh, and Kathy wasn't mine to be jealous of anyway.

Marcella's eyebrows rose high on her forehead, then she gave me a mocking smile. In the corner of my eye, I saw Kathy wipe off her mouth while my best friend and I engaged in a stare off.

"So Kathy...," Marcella started, her eyes still locked onto mine. "Are you dating anyone right now?"

We both turned towards Kathy expectantly.

"No."

"And do you date men, women, or both?" Marcella continued.

"Obviously she dates women if my mother tried to fix her up with me," I said in my best *duh* voice.

"It's not obvious at all," Marcella corrected, arching one eyebrow. "I doubt if your mother could pick a lesbian out of a line-up even if they were wearing a shirt with a rainbow flag on it."

It was true. My mother tended to operate in her own little world. If something wasn't about our family or our business she didn't have a lot of curiosity about it.

"I mentioned it," Kathy interrupted. "I remember her asking me what I meant when I said that I wrote sapphic paranormal romantic comedies and after I explained all the terms to her, she asked how I know how...," Kathy made air quotes here, "everything worked for my lesbian characters, and I said it was because I *am* a lesbian character."

"And then she told you she had a daughter who was a lesbian?" Marcella asked.

"Oh no, for the next few weeks every time I saw her she went on at length about how she'd love to have me come over and discuss my books more. Since I knew she obviously wasn't one of my target readers, I assumed she was lonely or something and eventually she wore me down."

Kathy shot me a quick look.

"I was surprised when Ava was there. And her father."

And I treated her like crap, I added silently.

"Since you're single and on the market..."

"She didn't say she was on the market," I interrupted Marcella.

Kathy's gaze bounced between us curiously.

"Maybe you'd like to go out with us sometime," Marcella continued. "There's a great lesbian bar that Ava and I go to from time to time not far from here. They have live music on the weekends and a huge rooftop patio where you can lounge around and talk to people."

"That's nice of you Marcella," she said, "but probably not a good idea."

"Why not?"

Kathy inclined her head towards me, and I felt guilty.

"Oh, well we don't have to go with Ava," Marcella rushed to add. "The two of us could check it out one night. Together."

I studied my best friend, trying to decide if she really liked Kathy or if she was hitting on her just to annoy me. Knowing my best friend, it was probably the latter. But then again, she was always looking for some easy and uncomplicated sex, so maybe not.

"I'll go," I said quickly.

They both turned to look at me as I strove to act casual.

"I think you and I got off on the wrong foot, Kathy. I'd love it if you would come out with me and Marcella sometime. I owe you a drink."

"I don't know…"

I didn't know if her hesitance was because she didn't want to go, or if she didn't want to go with me.

"You said you spend too much time in your…what did you call it? Your writing cave?"

At her nod I continued. "Well, let's get you out of the cave and have a fun night on the patio, what do you say?"

Kathy's eyes bounced between me and Marcella as she considered the invitation.

"Okay, yeah, thanks, that sounds fun," Kathy agreed.

I breathed a sigh of relief. "Great, why don't you give me your cell phone number."

CHAPTER EIGHT — UP ON THE ROOF

Two months later...

"Whatever happened to that hot girl?"

I pressed my drink against my forehead to cool off and looked at my friend Marcella across the table. We were hanging out on the rooftop terrace of our favorite lesbian bar. In the far corner, a calypso band was keeping things lively enough that a few brave souls were dancing despite the fact it was ninety-nine degrees and about a million percent humidity. I leaned closer to the airflow of one of the giant fans that was moving the hot air around on the rooftop. It was twilight, but the heat showed no signs of abating. Welcome to summer in Chicago.

"We should have sat inside," I said. "I'm melting out here."

"It's hotter inside," Marcella replied. "The AC can't keep up with this damned weather. So...the hot girl?"

"What hot girl?" I frowned.

"Remember in the beginning of the summer we went to the beach, and we ran into that girl your mom tried to fix you up with, the one with the great tits?"

"Ah yeah," I said, acting like I didn't know who she was talking about the minute she asked. "Kathy. She ghosted me."

"Ghosted you?" Marcella asked, as if she'd never heard the word before.

"Ghosted me. Well, blew me off, I guess. After we saw her that day I texted her – twice – and she never replied. Can't get any clearer than that."

"I should have called her," she said. "That girl liked me way better than you."

"Did not," I argued weakly.

"Did too." Marcella pulled out her phone. "Give me her number."

"I don't think I have it anymore."

She pinned me with a hard stare.

"Ava Rachel Morganstein, I've known you since you were a tiny girl. I can tell that you're lying. The question is...why? Are you afraid she's going to like me better? Because let's face it, everyone does."

I sighed. "Fine."

I pressed a couple of buttons on my phone to send the contact to Marcella. Her thumbs flew across the screen as she texted Kathy. Not thirty seconds later her phone beeped with an incoming text.

"It's her!" Marcella said, giving me a triumphant smile.

She tapped out another message.

"What are you saying?" I asked curiously.

"I'm asking her if she wants to come join us for a drink."

"What?" I yelped, pointing to my limp hair and sweaty face. "I look terrible right now!"

"You said you weren't interested in her," Marcella reminded me. "So why do you care?"

"Just because I'm not interested doesn't mean I want someone to see me looking like a rat that's drowned in its own sweat."

"Yet you don't mind a bar full of queers seeing you like that."

I sent her a stern glare. We'd been friends since kindergarten, which meant that we knew each other too well. After I came out as a lesbian and Marcella came out as bi, I'd often thought it was too bad that we weren't attracted to each other since we had such a great relationship. Most of the time.

I couldn't figure out if she really was interested in Kathy, or if she was just poking me about her. More likely the latter. She'd probably figured out that I was attracted to Kathy and was trying to push me into doing something about it.

Not that I could.

Kathy had been pretty clear that she thought I was a jerk, and even though I was a grown woman, I was not going to give my mother the satisfaction of dating one of her fixups. When Kathy and I broke up – which we inevitably would – I'd never hear the end of it. Plus if she knew she picked well, Mom would just be emboldened to continue her matchmaking until she had me married off.

Twenty minutes later I felt a little prickle on the back of my neck. When I looked up, I saw Kathy walking across the roof top terrace, garnering several looks of interest that she seemed completely unaware of.

She was wearing a short red sundress that hit her mid-thigh and a pair of flip flops. The dress was loose fitting and tied at the shoulders. I could tell by the gentle sway of her breasts as she walked that Kathy wasn't wearing a bra. My own nipples tightened in response.

Damn, she looked good. And a significant portion of the lesbians on this terrace agreed with me.

"Hey." Her voice was soft and sweet as she greeted us. "Thanks for inviting me, Marcella. I really needed to get out."

I bit my tongue to resist asking what else she might need that I could help her with.

Marcella patted the bench next to her.

"Have a seat, we were just about to order another pitcher of margaritas. You can tell us all about what's new with you."

CHAPTER NINE --
AUTHORPRENEUR

Kathy gave the server a smile as she brought another glass and a fresh pitcher of margarita. Manny blatantly checked her out, her eyes drawn to the top of Kathy's dress where I realized she was probably able to get a good view of Kathy's boobs. I ground my teeth and resisted the urge to punch her.

Manny had been a server here for as long as I could remember, and I had no doubt she could kick my ass. She was a fifty-something masc with a thick but muscled body and a crew cut. As usual she was dressed in combat boots and a white tank top, although in a nod to the heat her usual black jeans were cut off just above the knee.

"How have you been, Kathy?" I asked, drawing her attention from Manny.

"Not bad, but super busy. I just sent a manuscript for my next book to my editor like fifteen minutes before you guys texted. I realized I hadn't showered in a couple of days or – you know – been outside at all, so when my phone beeped as I was getting out of the shower I said to myself, go out among the land of the living, Kathy."

My brain hitched on the part where she was in the shower. My brain was apparently a pervert.

"So you're on a break for a while then?" Marcella asked.

"Well, not exactly. I'll start working on outlining and researching my next book until I get the manuscript back, then I'll do a couple of rounds of edits before it's ready to be published."

"I thought you were self-published?" Marcella asked. "Don't you just type something up and publish it?"

"That's a big misconception," Kathy said. "Self-publishing doesn't mean unprofessional. Some of the biggest writers in the business are self-published. E.L. James, Colleen Hoover, Lucy Score, they all hit it big while self-publishing. In fact, a lot of bigger authors like Brandon Sanderson are moving to self-publishing now."

"Why is that?" Marcella asked.

"You have more control over your book and its marketing. Your readers don't have to wait two years for the next book in a series. And frankly, if you do well in self-publishing you make more money than you would with trads. A traditional publishing deal you might get six to ten percent of the royalties, where if you self-publish you generally get about seventy percent. If you sell a lot of books, that really adds up."

"Wow, I had no idea." Marcella said.

"The bad thing is then you're responsible for everything, right?" Kathy continued. "You have to be what we call an *authorpreneur*. So I have a person who does all my social media and graphics, I have two editors, I own special formatting software, I run my own ads, and I have to do my own bookkeeping. But I wouldn't have it any other way."

"You make enough to write full time?" I clarified.

"I do. I'm one of the lucky few."

I held up my glass. "Congratulations on your success and congratulations on finishing your latest book."

Kathy and Marcella picked up their glasses so we could all clink them together for the toast.

Kathy looked between us. "I know you work for your parents, Ava." Her tone indicated that she wasn't impressed by that. "But what do you do, Marcella? I don't think we talked about it that day at the beach."

"Probably because we all drank some wine and fell asleep in the sun," Marcella laughed. "I'm a social worker. I work at a nonprofit organization that provides services to families exiting homelessness."

"Wow, that's an admirable career," Kathy told her, obviously impressed.

"It's hard work, but I like it," Marcella said. "Oh that reminds me, our big fundraising banquet is coming up in a few weeks on Saturday the twenty-fourth. I always bring Ava as my plus one, but this year I got an extra ticket. You should join us, Kathy. It's at the Art Institute."

"Oh, that sounds fun," Kathy said. "I haven't gotten dressed up for anything in a long time. Would you mind if I come too Ava?"

I gave her a smile. "No, not at all. Marcella and I clean up pretty well."

"Can't wait to see that!"

CHAPTER TEN -- DANCING IN THE HEAT

"Jeez, when is it going to cool off?" Marcella whined.

"Fall?" I suggested.

"I would smack you but I'm too hot to move."

I gave her a smirk and Kathy looked between us curiously. "You two never dated?"

Marcella and I both burst out laughing. "God no!" we said in perfect unison.

"Hmm."

"Hmm what?" I asked.

"You act like an old married couple."

"Well, we've been best friends since kindergarten," I explained. "We probably know each other a little too well."

The microphone squealed as the band came back from a break. "Next we're going way back to the sixties with *Dancing in the Streets*," the lead singer announced.

"I love this song!" Kathy said happily.

"Me too." I hopped up and grabbed her wrist. "Let's dance."

"Are you coming, Marcella?" Kathy asked as she got off the bench.

"Nah, I'll save the table."

I kept hold of Kathy's wrist until we got to the small dance floor. It was hot and crowded but we dove right in, dancing to the old song by Martha and the Vandellas. We bounced around to the beat, and when someone knocked into me from behind, I clasped my fingers together around Kathy's neck and moved closer.

She didn't punch me, which I took as a good sign.

"I'm glad you came out with us tonight," I called, leaning close to Kathy's ear so she could hear me. "It's nice getting to know you better."

"Even if your mother likes me?" she teased, but there was no malice in her tone.

"Well, she can't be wrong all the time," I joked.

The music changed, a slower song coming on. Without conscious thought, I pulled Kathy closer until only an inch or two separated our bodies. The sky was completely dark now, the terrace lit by a series of hanging lights that criss crossed the space and ran along the half wall that kept people from plunging off the side.

It was hot and sticky up here, yet somehow also romantic. Or maybe that was just because I finally had Kathy in my arms.

I reminded myself that if I hadn't acted like a jerk the first time we met, I could have gotten to this position much earlier. As determined as I was not to like her, there was something so compelling about Kathy. She was smart and funny and a little nerdy, a combination that was total catnip for me.

We swayed together, and when Kathy slid her hands around to grip my waist, I called it a victory. I looked at her face, taking in the way her dark hair was turning curly in the heat, and the fine sheen of perspiration on her pale white face. Her large brown eyes met mine, and our movements slowed.

Neither of us spoke, as if by unspoken agreement we tried not to break the spell.

My heart was thudding painfully in my chest and my core felt heavy as my body became more and more aware of the woman in my arms. I chanced a look down, getting an eyeful of the slopes of her breast that were visible beneath her loose sundress. I had a sudden urge to untie the string on her shoulder and bare her breasts so I could suck them into my mouth. The image was so strong, I could feel a flood of arousal rushing through my pussy. If my panties weren't already soaked from the heat, that would have done it for sure.

I pulled her closer, my breasts lining up right above hers.

"What are we doing?" Kathy whispered.

"Just dancing," I replied. "For now."

CHAPTER ELEVEN – DOUSING THE FIRES

"Did you two have a nice dance?" Marcella smirked when we returned to the table. "Y'all looked pretty cozy over there."

I sent her a warning look that she ignored. Meanwhile, Kathy was ignoring my gaze, making me wonder if she regretted us getting so cozy on the dance floor. She'd been turned on too, I was absolutely sure of that.

"It's almost last call," Manny came to our table with her order pad and a bored expression. "You want anything else?"

"Another pitcher of margaritas please," I said politely.

"And can we get some water, too please?" Kathy asked, looking up at her with those huge doe eyes she had.

Manny gave her an indulgent smile. "Sure thing, sweetheart."

Marcella and I looked at Kathy in shock.

"How did you do that?" I whispered as Manny left. "Are you a witch or something?"

"What are you talking about?"

"You made Manny smile," Marcella said, her voice awed. "We've been coming here for years, and I never saw her so much as smirk."

Kathy rolled her eyes. "Come on."

"We're not joking," Marcella replied in a sing song voice.

We lapsed into silence until Manny came back with our drinks, dropping the check on the table without another word. The three of us rummaged around in our wallets, pulling out cash as we sucked down more margarita and then gulped some water. I should have had a nice buzz going by now, but with the heat I swear I was sweating off the alcohol as fast as I was drinking it.

"I'll email you both the information about the gala," Marcella said as we got up to leave. "We can all meet at the Art Institute if that works."

"Sounds good," I said, even though I knew she was saying it for Kathy's benefit. I would see Marcella several times between now and then. It was rare that even a week went by without us seeing each other.

We walked through the roasting hot bar and down the stairs to the street. It seemed hotter down here, with heat radiating off the sidewalk despite the late hour.

"I'll see you gals later," Marcella said, turning in the direction of the elevated train station a few blocks away.

"Wait, no way, you're not taking the El at this time of the night," I protested. "Take an Uber."

She gave me a look that reminded me that Ubers were expensive, and she made subsistence wages as a social worker. It was ridiculous really that Marcella's job was so much more stressful and important than mine, yet she made a fraction of what I did.

"I'm calling you an Uber," I said firmly, already typing in her address in the app. "It's going to be gates of hell hot on the train. A nice car with AC will be much better. It's my treat."

A flash of uncertainty crossed her face, and I moved closer, whispering in her ear, "Take the fucking Uber, Marcella. It'll make me feel better to know that you're safe."

"Okay then," she said, giving me a quick hug. "Thank you."

"What about you?" I asked Kathy. "Where do you live?"

"About ten blocks from here," she said, pointing north. "Close enough to walk."

"I'll walk you."

"If I take an Uber and you walk Kathy, how are you going to get home?" Marcella said, raising her eyebrows at me.

"By the time I walk Kathy home you'll be dropped off and I can order my own Uber."

Just then a car pulled up and after verifying it was the right driver, Marcella slid into the back seat, sighing loudly. "Blessed AC!"

We watched her drive off, then headed in the direction of Kathy's house. We were both silent as we walked through the mostly empty streets.

"This is me," Kathy said, pointing at a brick six-flat.

"Nice place," I said, admiring the nicely manicured front lawn and wrought iron fence around the property. "Do you own or rent?"

"Own."

Another way we were different. I lived rent-free in a place my parents owned while Kathy had turned her creative pursuits into enough of an income to afford to buy a house in an expensive city.

She turned to face me. "Thanks again for tonight, and for walking me home."

"It's no problem."

I stepped closer, wondering if I should kiss her, watching her face carefully for a sign that it was okay to make the next move. Kathy swayed towards me, just the slightest, and I lifted one hand, intending to cup her cheek.

Suddenly thunder cracked, making us both jump, and then the skies opened up, sending a deluge of rain down before we took our next breath. We both looked up towards the sky, then laughed.

"I'd better get inside," Kathy said. "Good night."

I was looking for a sign, I guessed I got one.

Chapter Twelve — Texting Marathons

I waited exactly twelve hours after dropping Kathy off in the rainstorm before I texted her. Maybe I should have been playing cool or something, but it felt like we'd had a little breakthrough last night at the bar, and I didn't want her to retreat into her cave and never hear from her again.

I'd spent several restless hours thinking about her when I got home. It had been after three when I finally fell into a restless sleep. As I made myself coffee the next morning, I pondered the Kathy situation. How had I gone from indifferent to obsessed in only three meetings?

I'd been mildly attracted to her at my mother's house that day, but too annoyed to really admit it. At the beach I'd felt attraction hit me harder, but I was still determined to ignore it – not because of anything about her, but because of my mother's involvement. But last night...talking and laughing with her, holding her in my arms while we danced...it all felt different.

Suddenly I didn't care that my mother tried to fix us up. I didn't care that Marcella may or may not have been attracted to her too. All I cared about was figuring out if she was feeling the same jumble of attraction and fascination that I was.

So I texted her.

> **Me:** Hey there. I had fun hanging out with you last night.

After I pressed 'send' I stared at the phone screen like a loser for a full five minutes. My heart started thudding in my chest when I saw the little dots dance across the screen, telling me that she was composing a reply.

> **Kathy:** Yeah, thanks again for inviting me.

Hmm. That seemed kind of neutral. I waited a few minutes before typing again.

> **Me:** Would you like to go out with me some time?

I decided to put it all out there. As soon as my message sent, the dots danced across the screen. And danced. And danced some more. I worried my lower lip between my teeth as I waited for Kathy's reply.

It was weird. I normally wasn't particularly invested in things like this. I didn't fear rejection – not that I got rejected a lot anyway given that I was reasonably attractive, and most people knew who my family was. I'd always figured if one woman said no, there was always another woman.

Except I didn't want another woman. I wanted Kathy.

I jumped as my phone pinged with a new message.

> **Kathy:** Like a date? Or as friends?

I sighed. I supposed my initial tepid response to her made her confusion understandable.

> **Me:** My preference is a date. But if you aren't ready for that or you aren't attracted to me, I'll settle for friends.

> **Kathy:** A date is good.

A smile broke out on my face. She was willing to go out with me! It felt like a second chance, one I shouldn't mess up.

> **Me:** How about tonight?

> **Kathy:** Oh sorry, I'm actually on a train right now heading out of town.

People still took the train for long trips? I had no idea. Maybe Kathy didn't drive. A lot of people who lived in the city never got their licenses.

> **Me:** Where are you going?

> **Kathy:** I'm going to Indianapolis to visit my family. It's my mother's sixtieth birthday and we're

having a big party for her tomorrow.

Me: When do you get back?

Kathy: Next Saturday afternoon. There's so family drama I need to help with too.

Me: Can you have dinner Saturday when you get back?

Kathy: That sounds good.

We spent the next week compulsively texting. Or maybe that was just me who couldn't put the phone down. All I knew was that we scarcely went two hours without one of us texting the other. Despite the limitations of text we had long conversations about our dating histories, our interests, our families, and what we were looking for in a relationship. Even though we were different in many ways, we had a lot more in common than I would have expected.

By the time Saturday rolled around I was on pins and needles waiting to see her. Wondering if she'd let me kiss her. I paced around my apartment, cleaning and checking my cell every two minutes to see if there was a new message from Kathy.

I was rewarded just before three o'clock when my phone pinged with an incoming text.

> **Kathy:** I'm back. Where shall we meet?

Chapter Thirteen – First Date: The Beginning

I'd been debating all week where I should take Kathy for our first date. Instinct told me to not go overboard, so I suggested that we meet at Murphy's Irish Pub downtown. The pub was a sprawling space on the bottom of a hotel near the Chicago River, surprisingly bright despite it being partially subterranean. The large windows that ran across the walls on three sides of the space helped.

I waited for Kathy in the lobby, standing between a framed jersey from Chicago Bears football legend Dick Butkus and a hockey stick signed by the 2015 Stanley Cup winning Chicago Blackhawks.

The door opened and I was glad I'd gone casual with jeans, a form-fitting shirt, and a pair of sandals that highlighted my sparkly purple toenails.

Kathy was wearing faded jeans that fit her like a second skin and a baby blue tank top with a cute blue and white checked shirt over it, untucked and unbuttoned. Her thick hair hung past her shoulder in a riot of curls, and her lips shone with a shiny red lip gloss.

We gave each other an awkward hug before heading to the hostess stand. We were seated in a corner booth underneath a giant Bailey's whiskey sign. That's what I loved about Murphy's – it was an eclectic combination of Irish and Chicago cultures.

We ordered beers and a soft pretzel that came with a beer cheese dip.

"How was your mother's birthday?" I asked.

Kathy chewed a bite of pretzel, looking thoughtful. "It was okay. It's just that...well, every time there's a family event I feel like I'm the loser of the family."

"How are you the loser of the family?" I asked in surprise. "You're a successful author."

"Being a writer isn't a sustainable career," she said, making her voice higher and judgmental as she imitated someone. "If you can't find a husband, you could at least get a career that will support you as you grow old."

"You're not out to your family?" I asked in surprise.

"Oh no, I'm out to them. I came out to them in college, but before that I dated the same guy for three years, so they assumed me saying I was a lesbian was just a knee jerk response to my heartbreak," she explained. "They're convinced that I'm only dating women to avoid having my heart broken again -- even though I'm the one who initiated the break-up – and when I find the right guy I'll come to my senses."

"Damn. That's rough."

"What about you, Ava?" she asked, her lips quirking up on one side. "You know it's not a proper first date in the queer community if you're not sharing your coming out story."

"Yeah," I laughed. "It was pretty anti-climactic. I think my mother had already figured it out by the time I told her, so she took it in stride. My father has very little interest in my personal life. He's more of a don't ask don't tell guy, and I don't mean that in the homophobic way, more that he doesn't ask anyone about their personal life and he's a vault about his own. Then again, Mom does enough sharing for the both of them."

"It sounds like we were both relatively lucky," Kathy said.

"Yeah, I guess we owe a big debt of gratitude to the previous generations who did all the hard work on LGBTQ acceptance."

Kathy held up her glass in a toast. "To the queer trail blazers."

"To the queer trail blazers," I repeated, clinking my glass against hers.

"Are you ready to order dinner?" I asked, tilting my head towards the waitress who was hovering a few tables a way, watching us.

"Yeah." She picked up the menu, studying it carefully, before she gave me a serious look.

"I have a proposal for you," she said.

"A proposal?" I repeated. "That sounds intriguing."

Chapter Fourteen – First Date: The Murky Middle

"What's your proposal?" I asked Kathy, hoping it involved her and me naked, and soon.

"We should order two entrees and split them."

"Huh?" As usual, I was extraordinarily eloquent.

"It's fine if you don't want to, but I hate choosing one thing to eat, so when I eat with my friends or sisters I usually try to get them to split entrees with me," she explained. "That way we both get two things."

"Hm, that's actually kind of a good idea. What should we split?"

After a little discussion, we ordered a corned beef sandwich with sweet potato fries and a shepherd's pie. When the food arrived, we shifted the food between plates until we each had half a sandwich, a handful of fries, and half of the shepherd's pie. The food was delicious, and we fell mostly silent as we ate.

As the silence dragged on, I got a little twitchy, feeling almost desperate to fill the empty space.

"Is everything okay?" I asked.

Kathy looked up with a confused look. "Sure, why wouldn't it be?"

She slid a sweet potato fry into her mouth and my attention fixed on her plump lips. Kathy had an unassuming beauty, the kind that you'd miss if you weren't paying attention but if you took a good look at her with her huge eyes, crooked smile, and cute little button nose, you'd realize she was a stunner.

Or maybe that was just me. I'd seen both men and women checking her out since we sat down.

"You were kind of quiet, I thought maybe I'd said something wrong or something," I said lamely.

I hated the way I sounded insecure. It was so unlike me. Yet ever since the first time I met her at my mom's, something about Kathy had thrown me off balance.

"I'm a very quiet person," she responded. "I spend ninety-nine percent of my time alone. Sometimes I go days without speaking to anyone. I'm afraid I'm not very good at small talk and peopling."

"You did okay the last few times I saw you," I reminded her.

"Well," she said, taking a small sip of her beer. "There was more alcohol involved, and we had Marcella with us. She's very... chatty."

That was a kind way to point out that my best friend pretty much never stopped talking. I was so used to her I guess I'd never noticed the way that she filled up any empty spaces with her chatter.

"I think it's because she listens to people's problems all day at work," I explained. "When she finally is free to express herself as she chooses, she goes all out."

"I'm better at texting than talking," Kathy said. "Don't take it personally, Ava."

We lapsed back into silence, and I snuck looks at her from beneath my eyelashes in between bites. When I finished my food, I asked the question I'd been dying to ask for a while.

"What do you have going on tomorrow?" I asked.

"My usual Sunday," Kathy replied. "Going to church, volunteering at the soup kitchen..."

"Really?" I asked in surprise.

Kathy burst out laughing. "No, I was kidding. I'll sleep in, do some laundry, watch something on Netflix, and if I get particularly energetic, I'll go grocery shopping."

"And if you don't?" I asked.

"Then that's why they invented food delivery."

"Well, thanks for having dinner with me," I said, "it was fun."

I figured that our date was going to wrap up after dinner. It was kind of a bummer, given how attracted I was to her, but at least I'd given it a shot. We seemed to be getting along fine, but there was no flirting or any indication that Kathy liked me as anything more than a friend, and despite her saying she was quiet, I wasn't getting a 'let's spend more time together' vibe.

Until she said something that I wasn't expecting.

"Do you want to come home with me and fool around?"

I stared at her in shock. "Really?"

Kathy nodded. "Yeah, you're hot as fuck and I could use a good fuck."

Chapter Fifteen – A Surprising Turn of Events

"Oomph."

I gasped as Kathy pushed me against her front door before I'd even taken two steps into her house.

We'd had a very quiet Uber ride to her place, each of us tucked into our side of the car, but once we got inside her house it was like someone had fired a starter pistol and Kathy was going for the win.

"I've been dying to kiss you," she said as she pressed her body against mine, trapping me between her and the door.

Her taking control was another surprise, but I didn't hate it. Kathy slid her fingers into my hair, cupping the back of my head, then leaned forward until our lips were so close I could smell the faint hint of beer on her breath. She stared into my eyes and, seeing whatever she was looking for, pressed her lips against mine.

It was just a slight press of skin against skin and yet it sent a jolt of pure adrenaline through my body. I gasped, and Kathy took advantage of my lips parting, sliding her tongue into my mouth. She explored me with a thoroughness that ratcheted up my arousal faster than I would have ever expected, but I was no passive participant.

I slipped my hands around her hips, cupping her round ass and pulling her closer as the kiss continued. My tongue dueled with hers as my heartbeat increased exponentially. I couldn't remember ever being this excited just from a kiss. It was crazy.

Kathy pulled away and we both dragged in a long, deep breath. She tilted her head, licking down the side of my neck to the juncture of my neck and shoulder. I gasped as she caught my flesh between her teeth, biting down just enough to sting before soothing that spot with her tongue. Meanwhile, her arms slid in between us and before I even clocked what she was doing, Kathy's hands were underneath my shirt. I moaned as her hands found my breasts, cupping them in her palms and giving them a firm squeeze.

"God, your tits feel amazing," Kathy whispered. "I want to suck them into my mouth and tease your nipples with my tongue while I fuck you with my fingers."

Wow, so Kathy was a dirty talker. I did not see that coming.

"What are you waiting for?" I gasped as she squeezed my breasts again.

"Oh no, you've got to earn your orgasm." Her voice was dark and surprisingly firm.

"How?" I asked, ready to do anything.

My nipples were painfully hard underneath her hands, my core felt heavy, and my panties were already soaked with arousal. I couldn't believe how quickly Kathy had ramped up my excitement.

She stepped back, grabbing my wrist and pulling me behind her. Her steps were fast and purposeful, and I practically had to jog to keep up with her. She led me back through the living room, past a dining room and kitchen I scarcely got a glimpse of, and down a hallway. We passed two doors on either side, heading for the door at the end of the hallway. The master bedroom.

It was a large room with a sliding glass door on one side, leading out to a balcony. In the middle of the room, a queen sized bed was pushed against the wall, the black wrought iron frame a contrast to the white comforter and matching pillows piled up on the bed.

"Get naked," Kathy ordered. "Now."

I'd never in my life been bossed around in the bedroom but damn, this was hot. I undressed quickly while Kathy only removed her outer shirt and shoes. Before I could ask when she was going to get naked with me, she pointed at the bed.

"Get on your back. I want to ride your face."

Chapter Sixteen — Oral Fixation

"Don't you need to get undressed to ride my face?" I asked saucily as I lowered myself down on the bed and situated myself in the center.

Without a word, Kathy grabbed the hem of her tank top. Slowly, so slowly, she slid the fabric upward, over her lower stomach, past her belly button, over her midriff. By the time she peeled the shirt over her breasts, I was panting in anticipation. She wore a plain white silk bra under her shirt, and it was the sexiest thing I'd ever seen. After tossing her shirt in the direction of the hamper in the corner, she reached behind her and unclasped her bra, releasing her heavy breasts.

They were shaped like tear drops, with large dark red areolas and prominent nipples that made my mouth water. Next her fingers went to her zipper, lowering it slowly before easing out of her jeans, teasing me with her deliberate slowness. When her fingers finally moved to the waistband of her panties, I was seconds away from screaming in frustration.

I needed to see her. I needed to touch her. And I needed to get off. But first I needed to take care of Kathy.

She strode proudly towards the bed, seemingly confident in her skin, then crawled up my body, stopping to give me a long, deep kiss. She propped herself up on her elbows and stared down at me for a long moment.

"Make me come with your tongue, and as a reward, I'll give you so much pleasure that you'll forget your own name."

I damn near came on the spot.

"Okay, yes," I croaked. "I can do that."

She smirked, amused at throwing me off my stride. "Good girl."

Another flood of moisture rushed to my pussy.

Popping back up on her hands and knees, she continued moving up my body until her core was lined up with my face. I glanced up, watching as she shifted to kneeling and grasped the wrought iron bed frame in her hands. Her pussy hovered just above my face, pink and glistening.

"Are you ready?" she asked, her voice suddenly husky.

"Yes, give it to me," I said. "I want to taste you."

She made a sound of approval before lowering herself over my face. I grasped her hips, pulling her down more, and licked along her labia before slipping my tongue into her channel. She tasted sweet and salty, and I eagerly lapped up her cream, licking her from bottom to top, pausing each time to tap along the edge of her clitoris with the tip of my tongue.

"More pressure," Kathy ordered from above me.

I immediately obliged, pulling her down a little more until I was surrounded by her, and then I flattened my tongue and explored the folds of her pussy with long, rough strokes. I moved one hand around, using my thumb to strum against her clit. Then I licked my way up inside her opening.

"Yes Ava, right there," she gasped.

Kathy started riding my face in earnest, rolling her hips and panting as she sought release. Blindly I reached one hand up until I reached her breast. I gave her a hard squeeze, and when she moaned I did it again, catching the tip of her nipple between two fingers and pinching as I continued to knead her flesh.

"Oh my.....fuck!"

Kathy's body stiffened, then she started shaking as she rode the waves of her orgasm. I released her breast and dug my fingers into her hips, keeping her close to my face so I could extend her pleasure with my tongue. She came so hard I couldn't keep up, and her cum trickled down the sides of my face.

With a long, shuddering sigh she moved off me, flopping down on the bed next to me with her arm flung over her eyes. Turning to my side, I propped myself up on my hand and licked her moisture off my lips. When I glanced back at Kathy, she was watching me with wide eyes.

"Wow," she said. "You really earned yourself a good orgasm."

CHAPTER SEVENTEEN – THE BEST "O" OF MY LIFE

I thought for sure that Kathy would need some recovery time after I'd wrung that orgasm out of her, but she apparently wasn't one to waste time. Pressing one hand on the front of my shoulder, she pushed me down onto my back and covered my body with hers.

Lowering her head, she gave me a long hard kiss, her fingers tangling in my hair to hold my head in place. Her dominant behavior in the bedroom was such a contrast from her introverted and easy-going behavior in the outside world. I loved the dichotomy, and I loved feeling like I was seeing a side of her that most people didn't get to see.

Kathy slid down my body a bit, nipping along my collar bones before lowering her head and wrapping her lips around one of my breasts. When she sucked it inside her mouth – or as much as she could take inside anyway – I felt a rush of arousal flood my core. I pressed my thighs together, desperate to prolong the pleasure.

"Kathy," I gasped.

She popped off my breast. "Sensitive breasts?" she asked.

"Yeah."

"Good."

Her smile was almost feral as she turned her attention to my other breast, sucking it hard enough to give me a bite of pain. I cried out as the pain turned to a pleasure that zinged through my body.

Slowly, so slowly, she licked her way across my belly and down to my hips. Bypassing where I needed her the most, she made her way down to my ankle, came back up my inner thigh, then jumped to the other thigh and made her way back up to my belly. Clearly she was trying to kill me.

I grabbed a hunk of her hair to get her attention. "Kathy! I need you."

She gave my pussy a little smack that made me gasp, quickly followed by another rush of arousal flooding my folds.

"Be patient."

Kathy shifted, then licked along the creases of my thighs before finally running her tongue along the outside of my labia. She sucked part of one of my labia into her mouth, biting down gently, then crossed over to do the same on the other side. No one had ever done that to me before. It felt incredible. I moaned softly.

Finally, finally she gripped me with both hands and spread my lower lips apart, revealing the soft folds on my pussy.

"Beautiful," she said almost reverently.

She licked up my channel and when I shuddered with pleasure, she did it again. Then, like a heat-seeking missile she sought out my clitoris, tapping it rapidly with the tip of her tongue. Meanwhile Kathy pressed one finger against my opening, moving inside easily given how embarrassingly wet I was. She pumped her finger in and out rapidly and I raised my hips to meet her, fucking her hand as waves of pleasure rolled through me.

I cried out as she added a second finger, her movements turning rough. I loved it. By the time she stopped tapping my clit, I was teetering on the edge. As if she knew it, Kathy caught my clit with her teeth, biting it gently as she swished her tongue back and forth against the tip.

Kathy moved, and then I yelped as I realized that she'd taken her other hand – the one not currently occupied with finger banging me – and slid it underneath my body. She pushed between my ass cheeks, then pressed a finger against my forbidden hole.

That's when I lost it. I screeched as the strongest orgasm I'd ever had in my life hit me. I thrashed about helplessly, my back arching off the bed and my head whipping from side to side. I was gripping the comforter so tight my fingers cramped.

And still it went on and on, Kathy's fingers and tongue pushing me through, not stopping until I had a second orgasm. Or maybe it was the next wave of the first one, I had no idea. All of my focus was on the sensations coursing through my body, crying out in ecstasy until I collapsed on the bed in a puddle.

Chapter Eighteen – The Brush Off

When I woke up a few hours later, I was alone in Kathy's bed. The almost-full moon shone through a gap in the curtains. Frowning, I slid my hand over the sheet next to me. The fabric was cool. I sat up, feeling a little spacy between the out-of-body experience and my subsequent nap. I hunted around for my clothes, pulling on my panties and shirt, but leaving my bra and jeans on the floor.

Kathy's apartment was mostly dark. I stopped in the bathroom across the hall, then headed into the living room. The woman who'd rocked my world earlier was sitting on the couch, her legs spread out in front of her, a laptop on top of a lap desk. She typed furiously, chewing on her lower lip with intense concentration.

I watched her for a few seconds, but she seemed unaware that I was there.

"Hey." I kept my voice soft so I wouldn't startle her.

A frown creased between her eyebrows, then she looked up slowly.

"Oh. Hi. Are you taking off now?"

I glanced down at my bare legs, then lifted my Apple watch. "It's two a.m."

She raised her eyebrows like she wasn't clear what my point was.

"It's a little late to go home," I clarified. "I thought...well I assumed I was staying over."

"We didn't discuss that," she said. "I guess I should have woken you up earlier, but you looked so cute sleeping curled up in a little ball like a puppy. Still, it should be no problem getting an Uber."

I was woman enough to admit that her comments hurt my feelings. Not the cute as a puppy part, but the part where she was trying to get rid of me. I'd had casual encounters before, interludes that were all about the sex. But even when it was clear going in that it was a one night stand, I'd usually slept over. Or they had, depending where we were.

"Oh. Okay."

She studied me with her head tilted, like she was confused. "Is there a problem?"

"What we did before...it was incredible." I could hear the question in my voice.

"Yeah, it was really good. Just what I needed."

"I guess, I thought it was the beginning of something." I sounded lame to my own ears.

"Oh God, are you one of those lesbians who wants to move in on the second date?" she asked. "I thought we were on the same page that this was just sex. We don't even really like each other."

"We don't?"

It wasn't just that we weren't on the same page, we weren't even reading the same book.

Kathy sighed deeply, then pressed something on her laptop and closed the screen. After setting her computer and lap desk aside, she pushed to her feet. She was wearing tiny sleeping shorts and a tight tank top that made her nipples look huge. I was immediately aroused again despite my irritation.

"Ava," she said patiently. "When your mother ambushed us with that fix-up, you told me you had no interest in dating, and I told you I only wanted sex. What part of that wasn't clear?"

"The part where we've hung out several times since then and we texted and flirted, and I thought now we *could* be dating."

"This is why you should always go to their house not yours," she mumbled to herself.

Suddenly I was furious. I stalked out of the room, finding my pants and shoes and pulling them on. I stuffed my bra into my purse and pulled out my phone and turned on the screen so I could call for a ride. When I came back to the living room, Kathy was still standing right where I left her.

If I'd expected her to look regretful or ask me to say, I was sorely disappointed.

"Bye," I snapped, pulling the front door open. "Thanks for the orgasms."

CHAPTER NINETEEN -- AN ACCIDENTAL ENCOUNTER

Six weeks later...

"This event gets more crowded every year."

I sent my mother an indulgent look. "You say that every year, Mom."

"It's true every year."

My mom and I had been coming to the Octoberfest celebration at St. Alphonsus Church ever since I was a little girl. The popular celebration was billed as an authentic version of the popular German festival held in Munich each Fall. All around us there was singing and dancing, beer, and food. With the weather being warm and sunny today, it seemed like everyone in Chicago had come out for the event – including the woman who'd ruined me for other women and then tossed me aside.

"Oh look, it's Kathy."

Mom hadn't stopped talking about Kathy since that night last spring when she invited her for dinner. Apparently my mother ran into her frequently at some coffee shop they both went to, which was totally weird since it wasn't near either of their houses.

My mom raised her hand to wave and yelled, "Kathy! Kathy! Over here!"

I squeezed my soft pretzel and tried to fade into the crowd. Mom wasn't having it. She grabbed my wrist and dragged me towards Kathy.

"Fancy seeing you here," she said, releasing my wrist to give Kathy a hug.

"Hi Mrs. Morganstein, how have you been?"

Kathy gave her a genuine smile, but when she turned to me, her smile looked a bit forced.

"You remember my daughter Ava, don't you?" Mom asked.

Our gazes met, and Kathy's eyes bounced with amusement. "Yes, of course I remember Ava."

She turned back to my mother, and I felt the sting of rejection. We'd hung out together several times and I knew what her pussy tasted like. Would it kill her to say hello to me?

"Kathy. There you are."

We all turned as a younger woman walked up to us and wrapped her hand around Kathy's arm. She was model beautiful – tall and thin with perfect skin, shampoo commercial quality hair, and perfect white teeth. I hated her immediately.

"Who's this?" I asked, realizing a second too late that my tone was a little harsh. My mother gave me a curious look.

"Mrs. Morganstein, Ava, this is my friend Simone. Simone, Mrs. Morganstein and her daughter, Ava."

Simone gave us a friendly smile. "Are you enjoying the festival?"

"We just got here," Mom said. "We were just going to get a beer."

"Great, so were we!" Simone said enthusiastically. "Will you join us?"

Out of the corner of my eye I saw Kathy shoot her a glance. I opened my mouth to refuse the invitation, but my mother beat me to it.

"That would be great. Thank you."

I suppressed a sigh. I guess we were doing this.

The four of us walked towards a huge beer garden tent that was set up on one side, cordoning the space off from the rest of the festival to avoid serving minors. There was a short line, and my mother and Simone chatted amiably while Kathy and I stood silently on either side of them like bookends.

"So how do you two girls know each other?" my mother asked Simone, clearly trying to figure out if they were together.

I wanted to know the answer to that question myself.

"Oh, Kathy and I go way back," Simone said evasively. "But we've recently found each other again."

I leaned back to look at the side of Kathy's head. She was staring at the guys pouring beer and clearly wishing that the line would move faster. I couldn't figure out why she seemed uncomfortable. Was it because my mom and I were interrupting her date? Or maybe she felt guilty about how she'd treated me?

We hadn't had any contact since I stormed out of her house in the middle of the night. I'd considered texting her about a million times, but after talking about it ad nauseum with Marcella, my friend had convinced me that it would be pathetic to pursue Kathy, so I didn't. Clearly she wasn't interested, and I needed to accept that.

Kathy turned her head and caught me staring at her. I thought she'd look away, but instead she stepped back and gestured towards the exit with her head.

"Ava, can I talk to you outside for a minute?"

CHAPTER TWENTY – THE SURPRISE COUSIN

I followed Kathy outside the tent and around the back, where a narrow walkway separated the beer garden tent from another building. She stopped several yards away from the walkway, then turned to look at me.

"How have you been, Ava?"

I looked at her like she was nuts.

"How am I? That's what you ask me after giving me one of the best sexual experiences of my life and then tossing me out of your apartment like I was yesterday's trash?"

I hadn't realized how angry I still was about that night until now.

"I realized after you left that it may have been harsh for me to kick you out at two in the morning," she started.

I raised an eyebrow.

"Usually when I sleep with someone, I try to go to their house so I can get away after. But for some reason, I found myself inviting you to come to my house that night. Then we finished and you looked so cute sleeping in my bed, I couldn't bear to wake you up and tell you to go. I'm sorry."

"What are you saying?" I asked. "You never have sleep-overs?"

"Not really. Inevitably I get an idea for whatever book I'm working on, or I get stressed out because I'm on a deadline, and the person gets offended that I'm leaving them to go write, or they come out and start talking to me and mess up my flow. It's easier to control if I can easily remove myself from that situation."

I studied her carefully, something not ringing true about her words even though I was pretty sure she believed them.

"You have intimacy issues," I said as the thought came to me. "You like to run before the other person can run, isn't that true?"

A look of irritation crossed her face. "Look, I didn't bring you out here for some dime store psychology."

"Why did you bring me out here then?" I asked.

"To apologize."

"It's been, what, six weeks? You could have called or texted. Why are you just apologizing now?" I asked.

"When I saw your face earlier, when your mom called me over, I realized I'd hurt your feelings."

"What about Simone?" I asked. "Does she sleep over at your house?"

God only knows why I was feeling jealous of the woman dating the woman who'd used me like a tissue and thrown me away, but I felt the way I felt.

"Well yeah, but she's my cousin."

I narrowed my eyes. "That's not how you introduced her earlier."

"Yeah, it's this whole weird story. I knew her when I was a kid because we grew up in the same neighborhood. A couple of years ago she did one of those DNA tests on a lark and realized that her father wasn't her father, it was the man who lived next door to them. My uncle."

I stared at her. "Okay, that's kind of weird."

"Yeah, I have a feeling it's going to make the holidays a lot of fun this year. My aunt had no idea her husband was fucking their neighbor."

"Wow."

We lapsed into silence for several long moments, our gazes locked on each other. Finally Kathy cleared her throat and spoke.

"It was one of my best sexual experiences too," she said softly. "I haven't been able to forget that night, Ava. I was tempted to call you several times, but after I'd been so clear that it was a one night thing, I didn't want to be a clinger or something."

I stalked closer to her, and she took a step backward, and then another, until her back hit the brick wall behind her. I moved closer, placing my palms against the brick on either side of her head. Moving in closer, I stopped with my lips only an inch from hers.

"If we agree that it was incredible, don't you think we should do it again?"

Before she could answer, I crashed my lips down on hers.

CHAPTER TWENTY-ONE – AGAINST THE BRICKS

K issing Kathy again felt like finding something I'd lost. I felt simultaneously sad, relieved, and excited. I pressed my lips firmly against hers, then wasted no time biting on her lower lip, demanding entrance into her mouth.

My kiss was hard and a little aggressive, but Kathy gave it right back to me. Her tongue fought for control with mine and she slammed her hands against my ass, pulling me into her body and grinding our hips together roughly.

I moved one hand to the small of her back and slid the other between her head and the wall to keep her from banging her head on the brick. The rough surface scraped against the back of my hand, but I didn't care. I was too focused on this incredible kiss.

When it was clear we both needed to breathe, I pulled back, staring into her eyes for a long moment. She looked the way I felt – a little dazed.

"Wow," Kathy whispered.

"Yeah."

Then I surged forward, kissing her again. I caught a scent of strawberry from Kathy's shampoo right before our lips met. I'd never thought much about kissing before. It had always seemed like a means to end. But with this woman, I swear I could kiss her for hours.

I shoved my thigh between hers, the movement lifting her up on her toes the slightest bit, giving her some pressure right where I knew she needed it most. My entire body was buzzing with excitement, arousal flooding my pussy and soaking my panties.

A burst of applause came from somewhere nearby, probably from one of the dancing performances, reminding me that we were in a public place. Even though we were relatively sheltered back here, anyone could walk by and see us.

"Fuck," I moaned as I pulled back, my breath labored. "We'd better stop before we get arrested for having public sex at a family event."

The word family seemed to bring her back to the present. She slipped out from between me and way, smoothing her hair down and adjusting her shirt.

"Your mom and Simone must be wondering what's going on."

"Yeah, let's head back."

I was tempted to take her hand in mine, but I didn't know how she'd react. I also didn't want to have to explain it to my mother or her cousin, especially when I couldn't explain it to myself.

"Can we see each other again?" I asked, hoping that I didn't sound as needy as I felt.

"Yeah, text me."

I stopped walking and turned to face her. "No offense, but you don't have the best record with returning texts."

She rolled her eyes even though she knew it was true.

"Tell you what. If I don't text you back within a day, call me instead. I often ignore texts when I'm working, but I get so few phone calls, that'll at least get my attention."

"Okay."

We walked back into the tent. My mom and her cousin were sitting at a table, chatting like old friends while sharing a bowl of nuts. They'd thoughtfully purchased beer for the two of us while we were outside.

"Is everything okay with you two?" my mother asked, looking at us curiously.

It took everything in me not to bring my fingers to my lips. I had a feeling that if anyone looked too closely it would be obvious that we'd been making out. I could practically see my mother's mind racing, wondering what was going on.

"Everything is fine," I said. "We just needed to talk about...something."

"Marcella!" Kathy said a little too loudly.

"What?" my mother asked.

"Who's Marcella?" Simone asked.

"She's Ava's best friend. She asked me out and I wanted to talk to Ava about it."

It wasn't exactly a lie, but it wasn't completely true either, unless you counted Marcella's invitation to join us at the bar last summer. Well, and her invitation for Kathy to join us at the fundraising gala that she skipped after our night together.

I grabbed my beer stein and took a large swallow of ale.

"Wait, how do you know Marcella?" Mom asked.

"We ran into each other around town a couple of times when Marcella was with me," I answered for Kathy. "We, uh, all had drinks together once. And you know how Marcella is, she's always flirting with people."

"If you don't take her, Kathy, I will," Simone announced.

We all turned to look at her.

"You've never even seen her," Kathy reminded her cousin. "For all you know she's a hideous troll."

"Girl, I'm so desperate to get laid, I don't care what she looks like."

Simone paused, her eyes widening, then turned to my mother. "Oh, I'm sorry Mrs. Morganstein, I forgot you were here."

"That's okay, dear," my mother told her, clearly entertained by the conversation. "I just wish my own daughter would be that proactive in finding someone to love."

CHAPTER TWENTY-TWO — AN UNEXPECTED CALLER

I spent the next two weeks trying to get together with Kathy. To her credit, when I texted her she usually responded to me the same day, or at least by the following morning, but our schedules were not aligning. At all.

> **Me: How about dinner Friday night?**

> **Kathy: I have a dinner meeting with one of my freelance clients.**

> **Me: You have freelance clients?**

> **Kathy: Yeah, I have a few regulars I work with to keep money coming**

in between book releases. Saturday?

Me: I have plans with my mother
on Saturday, how about Sunday?
Brunch? Dinner?

Kathy: I need to write that day.

And so it went. I was in the middle of a particularly busy time at my job, and Kathy was busy at work on her next book, and I was starting to wonder if it was even worth it. I liked her a lot, and I'd fallen a little bit in love with her the night we had sex – okay more than a little bit – but we seemed doomed to miss each other. With Kathy being so hard to read, I wasn't even sure if she was as interested in me as I was in her anyway.

Until the night she called me out of the blue.

My phone rang at around eight o'clock on a Wednesday night. I nearly jumped out of my skin when I heard it, since I rarely received phone calls, and not on random weeknights. When I saw that it was Kathy, I smiled.

"Hey."

"Do you realize that we've been trying to get together for more than two weeks now?" Kathy asked without preamble.

"Yeah, it's crazy," I agreed.

"What are you doing now?" she asked.

"Sitting on the couch reading," I responded. "How about you?"

"I'm standing on your front porch with a pizza."

I sat up straighter and looked around, as if she could see me through the door. "Wait, you're here?"

"Yeah."

"How did you get my address?" I asked.

"Are we going to play twenty questions or are you going to open the door?" she asked impatiently.

"Oh sorry, be right there."

I scrambled off the couch and headed for the door, pulling it open to reveal the woman I was obsessed with. She was holding a pizza box, a six pack of beer balanced on top of it and looking the tiniest bit unsure.

"Can I come in?" she asked politely.

"Yeah."

I stepped back and Kathy laughed softly. "What are you wearing?"

I looked down, realizing I was wearing bright green dinosaur slippers that Marcella bought me as a joke one birthday – although they turned out to be warm and comfortable – pajama bottoms with red and pink hearts on them, and an old hockey jersey that fell to the middle of my thighs.

"I wasn't expecting guests," I sniffed, smoothing down my hair.

"Sorry, I thought it would be fun to surprise you." Kathy looked around. "Is the kitchen in here?"

I followed her into my kitchen, grabbing plates and napkins and gesturing at the kitchen table. Kathy set the pizza down, then pulled two cans of beer off the plastic ring, sliding one towards me.

"Thanks," I said as I helped myself to a slice of pizza. It was still hot and smelled delicious. "I only had a bowl of cheerios for dinner, so that is going to hit the spot."

"Great. I figure you can never go wrong with pizza."

We were both quiet as we took a few bites of our pizza.

"How did you know where I live?" I repeated my earlier question.

She looked slightly embarrassed. "I called Marcella and told her I wanted to surprise you."

"Well, you surprised me," I said amiably. "So is this a booty call?"

Chapter Twenty-Three— Another New Proposal

"Would you be opposed to a booty call?" Kathy asked, taking a bite of her pizza. "If that's why I was here, I mean?"

I tamped down a stab of disappointment.

"I guess it depends," I said, waiting for her to look up at me before I continued. "Is this a one and done? If we sleep together, are you going to disappear or withdraw again after tonight?"

As usual, her expression was unreadable.

"I guess it depends on the parameters we set going in."

Kathy's vagueness annoyed me. I tossed my slice of pizza onto my plate and leaned forward to pin her with a hard gaze.

"We're not negotiating a business deal," I said impatiently. "After our conversation at Octoberfest I thought maybe we were on the same page."

"And what page is that?"

"I know we both said we didn't want anything serious in the beginning, but I don't want a one-night stand or random booty calls anymore," I said.

"What do you want then?" she asked.

"I don't want to just run into you every few months. I want us to try dating and figure out if we want to pursue something serious. I want us to spend time with each other on a regular basis like a normal couple. I want to do mundane things like go grocery shopping or hang out talking while we wait for the dryer to finish."

"Is that all you want?" she asked.

"Well, that and more of that mind-blowing sex we had. I really liked that."

Kathy smirked. "Tell you what. Let me finish my dinner because I haven't eaten all day and I'm ready to drop. Then once I'm revived, I'll make you come your brains out and then we can talk more."

I picked up my slice and chewed slowly, considering Kathy's words. Then I sighed. Something about her response felt like she was still keeping me at a distance.

If she had boundaries and parameters, that was fine with me, but not if it meant we weren't on the same page. I didn't want everything to be just about sex. I didn't want to wonder when or if I was going to talk to her or see her again. We'd done that, and it wasn't enough for me.

"As much as I hate to say this, maybe we shouldn't sleep together. At least not right away."

Kathy choked on her beer, spilling it down the front of her shirt.

"Say what now?" she sputtered as she sopped up the liquid with a napkin.

I was already regretting my suggestion as I noticed that the spilled beer had made her thin white tee shirt translucent, clearly showing a pert nipple pressing through the fabric of the bra below. My own nipples hardened in response.

"I feel like I'm saying this all wrong," I said. "It's just that...you're very hard to read."

"I'm going to be honest Ava, I feel like you've given me a lot of mixed signals," Kathy said. "First you have no interest in me at all, then you want to be friends, then I thought we agreed to a one night thing to scratch an itch, but you got all butt hurt after that I didn't profess my love for you or something. Then I see you at Oktoberfest and you kiss the hell out of me in an alley. If I seem guarded around you or hard to read, it's because I'm having some whiplash here."

"That's fair," I acknowledged. "So let me say this. I was wrong to reject you out of hand at my mother's house. I was rude and immature. I know that we got off on the wrong foot, then we somehow jumped around between the friend zone to having sex to radio silence. But I think we can both agree that the attraction between us is crazy?"

I looked up and waited for her to nod.

"But I feel more than that. It's more than just attraction for me. Is it for you?"

She stared at her plate for a few seconds before looking at me again. "Yeah, I think maybe it is."

"Then can we start over?"

CHAPTER TWENTY-FOUR – NEGOTIATING TERMS

"I think starting over sounds like a good plan," Kathy said.

I released the breath I was holding in a huge sigh. Kathy looked at me curiously.

"What?"

"What, what?" I responded.

"Why did you sigh like that?"

I shrugged. "It's just so hard to read you that I wasn't sure if you were going to agree, especially when you came over here for a different reason."

She chewed a bite of pizza thoughtfully before responding.

"Just so you know, I didn't come here just for a booty call. I would have enjoyed it, sure, but the fact is...well, like I told you at Octoberfest, I haven't been able to get our night together out of our mind. But as we've been texting and not being able to connect the last two weeks, I realized it was more than that. I...missed you. I missed the way we were chatting and texting before we slept together, and I missed having you in my bed, even if it was only for a short t ime."

"I missed you too," I said softly.

"All I knew was that you weren't really interested in anything serious and neither was I, so it felt safer to keep you at a distance before I caught feelings for you," she explained. "I don't know what this is between us, but it definitely feels like more than just casual. So that's it, I'm putting all my cards out on the table here."

"Okay, well if we're going to date, it sounds like we both need to work on our communication skills."

We ate the rest of our pizza in companionable silence, then loaded our plates in the dishwasher.

"Do you want another one of these beers?" I asked, lifting my empty can.

"If it's cool to hang out for a while."

"It's cool," I said.

I went to the refrigerator, and she followed me, presumably to help me grab the beer, and when I turned around, she was standing about a foot behind me. She wasn't wearing anything special – jeans and a shirt – but somehow she managed to make it look hot as fuck.

Setting the two cans of beer on the counter next to the fridge, I closed the door and walked closer to her. Instinctively she took half a step back before stopping herself. Without a word, I placed one hand on her shoulder, one hand on the back of her head, and pressed my lips against hers. Kathy sighed, opening her mouth enough for her to press her tongue against the seam of my lips and sneak inside. The kiss turned hot as she took control, walking me backwards until my hips hit the counter.

I dropped my hand to her hips as she cupped my cheeks in her hands, kissing me deeply and rubbing her body against mine. Given how little time we'd spent together it was weird how much I'd missed this. For some reason, kissing Kathy was different than any of the other women I'd kissed. It wasn't just the passion, although I felt that too, it was more about this sense like we just fit together, in a way that I hadn't experienced before.

She rolled her hips against mine and I did the same, the motion bringing some friction to our clits despite the fact that we were both fully clothed. My panties were soaked, and I could feel my nipples pressing against the thin fabric of my jersey.

"Fuck." Kathy sighed as she pulled back.

I leaned forward, running my tongue down her neck and pushing her shirt to the side so I could suck on the soft skin at the base. She cried out as I bit down, adding suction, suddenly desperate to mark her as mine.

Then I pulled away and gave her a soft smile.

"Do you want to watch TV?"

"What?" she asked, looking just the tiniest bit dazed.

I knew the feeling. It was amazing that just one kiss could make me feel this aroused, this excited, but we'd agreed that this wouldn't be just a booty call. As much as I wanted to fuck her right now, I didn't want to give her a reason to disappear again either.

"Let's watch TV and cuddle on the couch."

Chapter Twenty-Five – Stick with What You're Good At

"Ooh, look at this rhubarb, I know a great fish dish to make with this."

I tried and failed to hide my grimace. "I hate fish."

"You can't possibly hate all fish," Kathy said. "There's such a variety of flavors."

"Well, let me put it this way, I've never tasted any kind of fish I like." I paused as I thought back to visiting a friend in grade school. "Wait, I had frozen fish sticks once as a kid at Marcella's house. That wasn't terrible."

Kathy sighed as she put the rhubarb back in the bin. "You have the tastebuds of a toddler."

I grabbed the rhubarb back and put it in our basket. "I'm willing to try your rhubarb fish, if it makes you happy."

"It'll make *you* happy when you taste it," she said, handing money to the vendor.

Apparently I was a farmer's market person now. It turns out that even though she ate nothing but takeout when she was on deadline, when she wasn't, my girl liked to cook. She'd introduced me to several great new dishes during the three weeks that we'd been officially dating.

"Let's grab some whitefish and I'll cook for you tonight," Kathy said. "But tomorrow I need to focus on getting some words on the page. You've been distracting me from writing."

"Not the way I'd like to be distracting you," I teased. "How far off are you from completing your book?" I asked.

"About twenty thousand words, maybe twenty-five, until I give the first draft a second pass. It's been going super slow for some reason."

We walked past the next vendor, stopping to look at apples before heading out towards where I parked my car.

"I'll make you a deal," I said as I pulled my seatbelt on.

Kathy looked up from pulling on her own belt. "What's that?"

"Once you finish your first draft, I'll eat you out."

Her eyes widened. We'd been doing some heavy duty necking since we decided to start over, but we'd carefully avoided doing anything that moved us past second base. I'd been horny as hell, especially since we'd both agreed not to get ourselves off while we were waiting, and my control was beginning to fray.

Then again, I'd been enjoying hanging out with Kathy and doing couple stuff. We'd fallen into a routine that seemed to work for us, hanging out on weekends and a couple of nights each week. We'd gone to the movies once, visited a fall festival on the North Side, gone for long walks along the lake front, and had countless dinners together. The enforced celibacy had given us a chance to really get to know each other and figure out how we could be as a couple, without the sex getting in the way.

Then again, I missed sex getting in the way. At least a little bit.

"What are you saying, you're ready for us to take the next step?" she clarified.

"I am when you're done with your first draft," I replied.

"What if I don't want you to eat me out?"

"Of course you do," I scoffed. "I'm really good at it."

"What if I want to tie you to my bed, your arms and legs spread wide, while I kiss and bite every inch of your beautiful body. And then, when you're begging for me – begging – I'll make you come, first with my mouth, then with my fingers, and then with the toy of your choice."

She clicked her seatbelt and leaned back in her seat with a satisfied smile. "That's the reward I want."

I stared at her, my mouth wide open, moisture flooding my panties. Damn, my girl was the queen of dirty talk.

"I guess I wouldn't mind that," I finally squeaked.

She gave me another smile. "Great, because that's something that *I* am good at."

Chapter Twenty-Six — A Reward for Hard Work

"I'm done."

The text hit my phone just after four o'clock on a Friday. I knew right away what Kathy was telling me. She'd finished the first draft of her book which meant we were finally – finally – going to have sex again.

I hadn't been with anyone in the few months, not since the last time we'd been together. I told myself that I was still smarting over the way she'd kicked me out of her apartment after and disappeared without a trace, but I knew it was about more than just my hurt feelings.

I'd talked about this at length with my best friend and Marcella agreed with me. My persistent lack of interest in women who weren't Kathy was mostly about my sneaking suspicion that she'd somehow managed to ruin me for other women.

Before I slept with Kathy, I would have told you that I'd had lots of great sex. And it would have been true too. But one night with Kathy had made all my previous sexy times fade into oblivion. There was great sex, and there was sex with Kathy, and they were not even close to comparable.

I called Kathy back rather than texting.

"Tonight?" I asked as soon as she picked up.

"Come over after work," she replied, "I'm cleaning up all the detritus from my writing frenzy."

I'd learned that when Kathy was in the writing zone she was non-communicative, anti-social, and lived on coffee and whatever food she could get delivered. Fortunately in a city as big as Chicago there were a lot of options. This time around we'd worked out that she would text me sometime between five and ten p.m. when she could take a break to talk to me. That system had worked out well. I never know if I'd hear from her at five fifteen or nine fifty-nine, but she'd made an effort to make herself available to me, and that meant a lot.

It also forced her to eat and wash up and brush her teeth, so I think it worked out well for her too.

"I don't have any clothes with me," I warned. "Just what I wore to work."

"You won't need any clothes."

I looked around the office, as if someone could hear my whispered conversation from across the room, but it was mostly empty. I didn't know where everyone was today – maybe they'd all snuck out to enjoy what would probably be the last nice weekend we'd have in a while – but I was glad not to have any prying eyes. As the daughter of the owners, people seemed to take an inordinate interest in everything I did. I could never just be 'one of the guys' at work, which my parents repeatedly told me was a good thing because it meant when I took over after they retired, the transition would be easier.

"Should I bring anything?" I asked.

"I'm going to grill on the balcony, I just got groceries delivered."

"Okay, see you tonight then," I said.

I wasn't sure how my girl would live without food delivery services. If this was forty years ago, she would drop dead over her typewriter. Instead, she pressed a few buttons and ordered her grub through the internet. Fortunately, she made good enough money with her writing that she could afford the upcharges from living that way.

Someday I hoped that we'd live together. I pictured us getting a place together that was large enough for her to have an office space to write, with a floor plan that ensured she wouldn't be disturbed while I used the rest of the house.

That's right, somewhere between my mother sneakily trying to fix me up with Kathy and these last few weeks of dating celibately, I'd fallen in love with Kathy. Fallen so deep that I was picturing our happily ever after in a place where she could write, and I could be around to make sure she ate something besides delivery burritos and Thai food.

I just hoped that Kathy was getting there too. I still struggled to read her, but something had definitely changed between us since we'd agreed to give each other a fresh start. I had a feeling that she cared for me even more than she let on. Or at least I hoped that was true because Kathy was it for me.

My phone dinged with a text as soon as I hun up and my heart started pounding frantically.

Kathy: I have a surprise for you.
Bring whipped cream.

Chapter Twenty-Seven – Grilling & Flirting

I freshened up in the bathroom at work -- reapplying deodorant, combing my hair, and swishing my mouth with mouthwash – then headed over to Kathy's house. It was impossible to get an Uber or a taxi during rush hour, so I took the El train, then walked the rest of the way over to her house.

There was one of those ubiquitous mini marts on the corner, this one run by a very sweet Korean couple, and I popped in to pick up whipped cream, an Entenmann's pound cake, and a six pack of beer. My mother always taught me not to come empty handed when going to someone's house for a meal.

Although if the night went the way I was hoping, my meal was going to be Kathy.

She was dressed in leggings and a long sweater that drooped off one shoulder, revealing a tank top beneath. I was pretty sure she wasn't wearing a bra. Her thick hair was still damp at the ends from her shower, even though the top had dried.

When she opened the door I set my bag down and held out my arms. "Congratulations!"

She stepped into my hug, pulling me close. "Thanks, I think it's my best ever first draft."

"Well that certainly deserves a celebration," I said, stooping to grab my shopping bag. "I brought beer and pound cake. And the whipped cream you asked for."

Her eyes darkened, but she didn't comment.

"Can I help with dinner?" I asked.

"I've got the grill going. How about you crack us open some beer and come join me?"

"Gladly."

I put the pound cake on the counter along with the whipped cream, then put four of the beers in the refrigerator. It was fuller than I'd ever seen it, probably because of her grocery order today. After rounding up a bottle opener, I popped the top off two bottles of pilsner and followed Kathy out onto the balcony that overlooked the backyard of her building.

It was a nice set-up, with the unsightly fire escapes running along the side of the building over the gangway between two buildings, and staggered balconies on the back side of the building. Kathy has something unusual in the city: a large backyard. Even though it was shared by all the residents of the building, it was still a nice oasis of green.

Kathy's balcony was large enough to fit two Adirondak chairs with a small table between them, one chaise lounge, several potted plants, and charcoal barbecue grill. Kathy had burgers and brats on the grill, as well as several foil wrapped packages.

"What's in the foil?" I asked, handing her a beer.

She gave me a smile. "One is asparagus, and the other is diced potatoes and carrots. I cut them up super small, so they'd cook with the meat."

"Sounds good."

I watched as she turned the brats and flipped the burgers with practiced ease.

"You look so sexy handling a grill," I teased.

She rolled her eyes, but her face flushed a bit like she was embarrassed.

Kathy was a funny mix of contradictions. She was a bit socially awkward, or maybe just super introverted, but I'd seen the way she interacted with her fans on social media and there she came across as friendly and outgoing. She didn't take care of herself very well when she was on deadline, but when she wasn't, she was all about healthy cooking and getting exercise. She acted shy and easy going until we were in the bedroom, and then her dominant side came through.

I had a feeling I'd be trying to figure her out until the day I died. And I'd do it happily too.

"You ready to eat?" she asked.

"You mean dinner?" I sassed. "Or your sweet pussy?"

Kathy reached around and gave my ass a quick smack.

"Do I need to punish you later?" she asked, her voice suddenly deeper and stronger.

"I hope you will."

Chapter Twenty-Eight– Getting Down to Business

"Everything was delicious, thank you."

Kathy smiled at me across the kitchen table. We'd both been hoping to eat on the balcony, but the temperatures were dropping rapidly. The dining room table was covered in books that Kathy was autographing for fans who'd supported a Kickstarter for her new series. So we were eating in the kitchen, which was fine with me.

Kathy's kitchen was warm and homey, painted in shades of yellow with lemon print drapes and potholders and a cute mid-century metal table and chairs, upholstered with a lemon motif.

We stood up to clear the table, and suddenly Kathy seemed to stand straighter.

"I'll load the dishwasher. You get in the bedroom and get naked."

I shivered at the dark command in her voice. "Your bossy side is coming out again, huh?"

She gave me a stern look, but her eyes were twinkling, letting me know that she didn't take it all too seriously.

"Get moving."

"Yes ma'am," I said smartly.

"I like the sound of that," she called after me as I left the room.

I made a pit stop at the bathroom, then headed into the bedroom. I made quick work of taking off my clothes, piling them neatly on a chair, then sitting on the bed. I felt a little awkward sitting there totally naked, and that only added to the excitement that had been steadily coursing through my veins ever since her text earlier today.

I crossed my legs, then uncrossed them, then leaned back on my elbows, unsure how to situate myself. Kathy seemed to be taking a long time loading a few plates into the dishwasher. The longer I waited, the more anxiety and excitement warred in my mind. I breathed a sigh of relief as I heard her go into the restroom, then head in my direction.

I sat up facing the open door with my knees pressed together and my back arched to make my boobs look perkier.

Kathy stopped in the doorway, her dark gaze taking everything in, her lips quirked up into a tiny smile.

"Good girl."

Damned if I didn't like this game we were playing.

She walked closer, her hands coming to my tits and giving them each a hard squeeze. I gasped as a combination of pleasure and pain coursed through my body. Then, to my confusion, she walked across the room. I realized what she was doing when she came back with several long scarves in her hands.

"Get in the middle of the bed," she ordered, her voice soft but firm.

I knew from last time that she liked being in charge but was okay ceding control too. That's why I didn't hesitate to comply. Kathy didn't want some submissive doormat, but she did want someone who would trust her enough to give up control. Only then would she trust you enough to give up her own control.

I was glad to give up control, as new of an experience as it was for me, because I knew that whatever she had planned for me I was going to really, really enjoy it. I'd had no complaints last time, that's for sure.

I scooted to the middle of the bed, and after making sure my neck was supported by the pillows, Kathy pulled one of my hands upwards, tying my wrist to the metal bedpost. She pulled on the scarf to make sure it was secure, then ran her finger between the fabric and my wrist to make sure it wasn't too tight. Then she did the same with the other hand.

I started to pant when she grabbed one of my ankles, pulling it away from the midline of my body and securing it to one of the metal posts at the bottom of the bed. When she grabbed my other foot, my legs spread widely. Obscenely.

When my legs were completely immobilized, Kathy stood at the bottom of the bed, looking up my body slowly, a self-satisfied look on her face.

"You look so beautiful tied to my bed," she said, her tone a caress. "I can't wait to taste every inch of your body."

"Yes," I gasped. "Do that."

"But first I'm going to punish you for making me wait so long to have you again."

Chapter Twenty-Nine— Enough Teasing

I gasped in shock as Kathy turned around and walked out of the room.

"Where are you going?" I called, pulling at my restraints.

There was no response. I was trying to decide if I should be getting nervous when Kathy came back in with a small bowl in one hand, the can of whipped cream I'd brought in the other hand. I'd assumed that the whipped cream was for dessert, but I had a feeling I'd been wrong about that.

She set both items on the bedside table, then pulled an ice cube out of the bowl.

"What are you doing?"

Kathy pivoted and smacked the side of my hip hard enough to sting. Her eyes danced with amusement even though her face was stern.

"Be quiet, or I'll flip you over and spank your ass red."

A rush of arousal flooded my pussy and Kathy chuckled as she saw it. It's not like I could hide it with my legs open so wide.

"Ah, maybe that's not a punishment."

Still holding an ice cube, she hopped up on the bed and straddled the top of my hips, the fabric of her leggings coming into direct contact with the top of my pussy and making me gasp.

Then I stifled a squeal as Kathy leaned forward and circled my areola with the rapidly melting ice cube. She circled closer and closer before rubbing it across my nipple. The pain was exquisite, my nipple hardening as she continued to tease it.

When the ice was nearly melted she leaned over to grab another cube, treating my other nipple to the same treatment. This time she waited until there was only a small piece of ice left, then popped it into her mouth with an evil smile.

"Kiss me," I begged.

Kathy lowered herself over my body and tunneled her fingers into my hair before kissing me deeply. Our tongues slid against one another, the kiss somehow both rough and tender.

When we were both breathing heavily she started kissing her way down my body, licking and nibbling at my skin until I was writhing beneath her. By the time she settled between my legs I was so desperate for her touch I was practically incoherent.

"Such a pretty pussy," she whispered, right before she gave me a sharp slap between my legs.

"Hey! What was that for?" I said indignantly, even as the sting turned into a red hot heat.

"Your punishment," she smirked. "But the thing is, I want you too bad to do anything but this."

She spread my pussy lips open wide and gave me a nice, long lick. My hips levered off the bed, and Kathy pinned them back down with firm hands before licking me again, over and over again. She alternated the pressure and speed, not missing a single centimeter in her exploration. It felt incredible.

My entire body was buzzing, and everything else in the room seemed to fade away, my attention one hundred percent laser focused on what was happening between my legs.

"Kathy," I gasped. "Please, I'm so close."

"I've got you, baby."

She slid two fingers simultaneously into my opening and started pumping furiously. My hips rose to meet her with every stroke until she shifted positions a bit, pinning me down with one shoulder while she caught my clitoris between her lips. My nerves there were super sensitive, even that tiny bit of pressure sensitive.

I made a strangled sound that could have been a plea to stop or a demand to go on, I couldn't say. I struggled against my restraints, but they held tight. Completely dominated, I had no choice but to let go. And so I did.

My mind started flying as pleasure filled every part of me. It wasn't an explosive orgasm, but somehow I felt it deeper, like a slow wave of sensation that grew with every breath and left me shaking and crying until it was over.

Kathy pulled back as I came down, then she looked alarmed as her eyes reached my face, seeing the stream of tears leaking from my eyes.

"Oh my God, did I hurt you? I'm so sorry."

She was unfastening my legs before I could get a word out.

"I'm not crying from pain, I'm crying from release."

She rubbed my ankles as she removed the scarf, then moved up the bed to unfasten my wrists. Kathy looked so freaked out that I grabbed her hand, waiting until her gaze returned to mine.

"You didn't hurt me," I said firmly. "I loved everything you did, except for one thing that I needed…"

"What's that?" she asked.

"I didn't get to return the favor. How about you sit on my face now and I'll show you? Then we can figure out what to do with that whipped cream."

CHAPTER THIRTY – THE DISCOVERY

S ix weeks later...

"Mmm, Kathy that feels so good."

My girlfriend – yes I was calling her my girlfriend now – had woken me up with her head between my legs and her tongue licking my pussy like it was her job. Not a bad way to wake up at all.

My fingers curled around the sheets, trying to keep myself grounded as Kathy slowly and deliberately worked me towards orgasm. After all the times we'd had sex over the last four weeks we knew each other's bodies as well as we knew our own. We couldn't get enough of each other.

The last month had been an adjustment for sure. Between my job and Kathy's writing, it took some finagling to find time to spend together. I'd learned to be patient about the way that if Kathy was deep in her writing zone, she would drop off the face of the Earth. We'd negotiated that when she took a break she'd text me, and if I didn't hear from her for a few days, I had permission to come bang on her door.

Then we'd bang each other to make up for the absence.

But Kathy had just finished her second round of edits and turned her manuscript over to her proofreader, so this weekend, she was all mine.

Kathy licked her tongue into my opening, sliding it in and out quickly while teasing my clitoris between her fingers. When she gave my little bud a squeeze, I fell over the edge, moaning in pleasure while I bucked against her mouth.

"Did you hear something?" I asked as Kathy slid up my body and snuggled into my side.

"Just the sound of you coming your brains out," she said smugly.

Before I could respond I heard a gasp. My eyes flew to the doorway where my mother was standing frozen as she stared at the bed.

"Mom!" I yelled. "A little privacy!"

"Oh, I'm sorry, I'll uh, just wait in the kitchen."

She hurried from the room, leaving me and Kathy alone again.

"Does your mother always pop in like this?" Kathy asked mildly.

She levered off the bed, looking around until she located the clothes she'd been wearing the night before. I opened a drawer and pulled out a pair of pajama pants and a sweatshirt, not bothering with underwear or a bra.

"She comes over unannounced from time to time," I acknowledged, "but usually she knocks. I think something's wrong. She looked weird."

"I'd better go home."

When she walked towards the bedroom door I grabbed her wrist, pulling her against my chest and crashing my lips against hers. I could taste myself in her mouth, which just made me more excited. But the excitement would have to wait. I needed to deal with my mother.

"She's not going to let you go without an interrogation," I whispered against her lips.

"Your mother saw me naked," she wailed. "I can't face her now."

"Don't worry, she saw more of me." I threaded my fingers in hers and started walking towards the doorway. "We might as well get this over with. You know she's going to want to gloat."

When we reached the kitchen my mother was sitting at the table, a bottle of water in her hand. Behind her I could see that she'd started a pot of coffee.

"Mother," I said in my coolest voice. "I don't recall inviting you over this morning."

My mother raised one eyebrow and gave me the 'don't fuck with me' look she'd been giving me since I was a toddler.

"I wasn't aware that I needed an invitation to visit a property I own."

Kathy pulled her hand away and looked at me with a slight frown. "Your parents own this place?"

She seemed disappointed.

"The *company* owns this place," I said, emphasizing the word. "It's a corporate apartment that is technically the property of all the company shareholders, of which I am one."

My mother rolled her eyes, but then clearly decided she had bigger fish to fry. And she knew who would be the easier nut to crack.

"So, Kathy. How long have you been dating my daughter?"

Chapter Thirty-One – A Shock to the Heart

When Kathy just looked between me and my mother, I took pity on her.

"Sit down and I'll get us all coffee."

I poured three cups, then brought over a carton of creamer before joining my mother and Kathy at the table.

"First of all, why did you just come in here, Mom? We've talked about this."

My mother had the good grace to look embarrassed.

"You didn't answer when I knocked so I assumed you were either out or sleeping. I came by to drop off this."

She handed me a giant plastic container that I knew even before I opened them would contain peanut butter chocolate chip cookies.

"I wasn't expecting to find you...canoodling."

Ignoring that comment, I asked, "What are you and Dad fighting about?"

My mother only baked on birthdays and when she argued with my father. It wasn't my birthday.

"He's so stubborn. I want him to go see a cardiologist about his high blood pressure and chest pains, but he refuses. Then when I try to convince him he tells me I'm being too controlling."

I opened the lid, grabbing a cookie before sliding the container towards Kathy. Out of the corner of my eye I saw her take a bite of the still-warm cookie. The blissful look on her face made me want to drag her right back to my bed and go for another round, but unfortunately we needed to deal with my mother first.

"Anyway, so we had a huge fight last night and he slept on the couch."

"Why wouldn't he just stay in one of the guest bedrooms?" I asked.

"To prove a point. Then he was a complete jackass this morning, so he went skulking out to play golf and I started baking."

We were all quiet for a minute as we drank our coffee.

"I'm sorry I interrupted you girls," Mom said with obvious reluctance.

Her habit of popping over unannounced was a point of contention between us. As was the number of times I came home to discover that she'd been in my place while I was out, even if it was usually to leave me baked goods or some little gift she'd picked up somewhere.

I really should change the locks, although in fairness the condo did belong partly to her as well. Not that it made her behavior okay. I was a grown woman. I needed my privacy. Obviously.

"So...." My mother drew the word out and pointed a finger at me, then at Kathy. "How long has this been going on? Since Oktoberfest?"

I shrugged.

"As you know, we ran into each other a couple times and we've, uh, hung out and casually, uh, gone out a few times."

I couldn't tell my mother that we'd had a few hook-ups before we started dating. I looked at Kathy again before answering.

"We've been officially dating for about six weeks."

Mom clapped her hands, a smile lighting up her face.

"I knew it! I knew you two would hit it off. I told you. Didn't I tell you?"

"Yes Mom," I said in a long-suffering voice. "You did tell me."

"How serious is it?" Mom asked.

"Not too serious," Kathy said.

My head whipped around to look at her as a stab of pain hit my belly. Things had been going so well for us since the night she'd shown up at my apartment with pizza. We'd taken the time to become friends, putting the physical aside while we did it, and then when we put the physical stuff back on the table, it had just added to the flavor of the relationship. Everything between us had been going great.

Or so I thought.

My mother looked between us, her brain clearly calculating. "You too looked super cozy cuddled up in bed for people who aren't too serious."

She gave me a long look, and despite my efforts to keep my expression neutral, I could tell that Mom saw the pain and anger that filled me at Kathy's flippant response. Mom pushed up from the table and took her empty coffee cup to the sink.

"Well, I'll leave you girls to your cookies."

She walked by, placing a quick kiss on the top of my head. "See you later, Ava. Nice to see you again, Kathy."

"You too," Kathy said faintly.

We sat in silence until we heard the door close behind Mom, then I whirled around in my seat to face Kathy.

"What the HELL was that?"

Chapter Thirty-Two – Unexpected Consequences

"What the HELL was that?" Kathy flinched at my outburst.

"What did you want me to say, Ava?"

I got up from the table and started pacing back and forth in the kitchen.

"I wanted you to say that we're together, that we're dating seriously, that we're in love."

"Are we in love?" Kathy asked. "We've never talked about that."

I stopped to stare at her. "Aren't we?"

She shrugged, evading eye contact. "I don't know. I like you. A lot. But I've never been in love before. I...I don't even know what that feels like."

I couldn't decide if I wanted to cry or scream.

"I thought we'd moved past this, past your intimacy issues."

She stood up, looking pissed herself now.

"I have issues?" she repeated incredulously. "You're the one that didn't want to give me a second glance in the beginning because you were so hung up on your mother liking me. You're the one who wanted to bring a U-Haul and move in after one night together. And you're the one who has all these *rules* for our relationship."

The word 'rules' came out as a sneer.

"Rules? What are you talking about?"

She counted off on her fingers.

"We couldn't have sex until we met your arbitrary deadline, you need to talk to me every day, it's always your decision where we sleep over, it's okay for you to need to cancel something for your job but when I need to cancel for my writing I'm somehow being unreasonable...for someone who likes to be controlled in the bedroom, you sure like to control everything outside of it."

My jaw dropped in shock, not believing that she saw me that way.

"And now I'm hearing the word 'love' for the first time?" she continued. "Well I'm sorry if I didn't read your mind. And I'm sorry if I didn't know what the hell you wanted to tell your overly involved super nosy mother about why we've been dating steadily for over two months, and she had no idea."

"I just haven't had time to talk to her about it," I said defensively.

"You work with her and see her every day. You go there for dinner every other week," Kathy reminded me. "You've had plenty of time to tell her. But you're still locked in your rebellious teen phase with your mother, and you didn't want to give her the satisfaction of thinking she was right about us dating. Even if she was right about us dating."

She took a giant, heaving sigh. "Unfortunately she was wrong about us working out long-term."

She stormed out of the kitchen, making me realize I'd never seen her truly angry before. I would focus on how beautiful she was with her eyes flashing and her cheeks flushed, but I was too busy panicking about the way she was jamming her feet into her shoes and looking for her purse. I'd never seen her look this angry before.

"Wait, don't go Kathy. Let's talk about this."

She ignored me, walking around until she located her purse on the floor next to the couch. She opened it up, making sure her phone was inside, then headed for the door.

"Kathy. Please. Wait."

My voice sounded choked as I tried not to start crying.

"No Ava. I'm done with this. You're not as ready as you think you are to have a relationship, and I deserve somebody who will love me the way I am."

"I do love you the way you are," I protested.

"Funny how you've never mentioned that to me," she said. "I'm going home. I'm completely behind on outlining my book because I let myself cater to your need to spend time together on your schedule."

Crap, I had no idea that had happened. I felt like an asshole.

"Can I call you later?" I asked, my voice small and soft.

"Please don't."

Chapter Thirty-Three— Enough Wallowing

I groaned as the sound of knocking penetrated the layers of blankets I'd pulled over my head. It was probably someone wanting to talk to me about God. The knocking turned into pounding. Closing my eyes, I willed them to go away. When the knocking finally stopped I let out a sigh of relief.

My reprieve was short lived. Thirty seconds later I heard someone open my front door and close it behind them none too softly. Oh no. It was either my mother or something far worse...

"Ava Rachel Morganstein! You get your lazy ass out of that bed right this instant!"

The blankets were torn away from me, revealing way too much sunshine for what was no doubt a cold day, and the stern face of my best friend.

"What the fuck, Marcella?" I grumbled.

I tried to pull my blankets back, but she held on tight as we engaged in a silent game of tug of war.

"How long have you been in this bed?" she asked, her nose crinkling in disgust.

As usual, she looked like she'd just stepped off the pages of some fashion magazine.

"Just today," I lied.

"Your mom said you've called in sick three days in a row, and that when she last saw you Sunday you were here with Kathy looking like you were about to have a fight."

"Well then, you're all caught up," I said sarcastically.

"You never call in sick to work. What happened?"

"Nothing," I sighed.

Marcella slammed her hands onto her hips. "Here's what we're going to do. You're going to go take a shower because you smell ripe. And I'm going to throw these gross sheets in the washing machine and start a pot of coffee."

"No," I protested weakly. "They smell like her."

"They smell like you were eating Dorito's in bed," she said, picking up an empty bag between two fingers. "Now get in the shower."

Grumbling, I dragged myself out of bed, grabbed some clean clothes, and headed for the bathroom. When I looked in the mirror I nearly screeched. My hair was a rat's nest, my eyes were puffy from crying, and I had a crease on my cheek from the pillowcase. I was also wearing the same clothes I'd thrown on Sunday morning when my mother popped in and caught me and Kathy snuggling naked in bed. With a sigh, I turned on the hot water and stepped under the spray.

Fifteen minutes later I'd thoroughly cleaned myself, brushed my teeth, washed my hair, and conditioned out the tangles. Once I was clean and wearing fresh clothes, I almost felt human again.

I could hear the washing machine running as I came down the hallway to the kitchen, where Marcella was sitting at the table with a cup of coffee. Without a word, she got up and poured me a cup.

"Sit," she ordered, pointing at the chair across from her. "I brought you some bacon and egg breakfast croissants from that place you like up the street."

Realizing that I was hungry for the first time in days, I tore open the package and took a bite, washing it down with a sip of coffee.

"Do you want to talk about it?" she asked in an uncharacteristically kind tone.

I shook my head, but said, "Yeah."

I took a few more bites of my sandwich then spilled the whole story. My best friend listened quietly until I was done.

"She's kind of right you know."

My head popped up so quickly I heard my neck crack. "Hey, whose side are you on?"

"Your side Ava, always. But Kathy had a good point," she said. "You do tend to avoid talking about your feelings, and you are a bit of a control freak."

"No I'm not," I said hotly.

"You totally are," she said. "You're the worst kind of control freak because you think you're not controlling yet you have certain expectations for how things should go, how people should act, how they should respond. Then you're disappointed when people don't meet your expectations."

"I don't see that at all," I said stubbornly.

"Let me ask you something. Let's say you were in Kathy's shoes. You reject her, then you practically want to move in after you sleep together, then you reject her again when she doesn't respond to that the way you want her to, then you get back together and set all these requirements for her. I mean, how is she supposed to feel?"

"I don't know," I said, violently ripping off a chunk of sandwich with my teeth.

"You love her, right?"

"Yeah," I sighed.

"Well then, you should figure your shit out and get her back before she moves onto someone else. Because y'all are adorable together. And I want you to be happy even if you are an emotionally stunted control freak."

"I love you too, Marcella."

Chapter Thirty-Four — The Grand Canyon

Two days of texting yielded no response from Kathy, although I wasn't sure if it was because she'd blocked me or she was too busy writing. I tried calling her once, but it went right to voicemail. I didn't bother leaving a message, knowing that she would see it was me who called. After a lot of internal debate, I decided to go over to her house Friday after work.

I stopped at the florist on the way over and picked up a bouquet of daisies, Kathy's favorite. By the time I got to her apartment, my heart was pounding with anxiety. Taking a deep, calming breath, I knocked on the door.

A minute later Kathy opened the door. As usual, she didn't look through the peephole, something I'd often nagged her about. This time I kept my mouth shut, especially because based on the look of annoyance on her face, I was pretty sure she wouldn't have opened the door if she'd known it was me.

"What?"

She looked a little disheveled, dressed in baggy sweats with messy hair and dark circles under her eyes. I couldn't tell if she was upset about our break-up or just preoccupied. She often looked this way after a particularly intense writing session. Her ability to disconnect and focus on writing was admirable. Well, except when it meant that she was ignoring me.

"I brought you these," I said, holding up the flowers.

She made no move to accept them. Her face was set in a hard line as she just stared at me with her arms crossed under her breasts.

When she didn't say anything, I spoke again. "Can we talk? Please?"

She shook her head. "Look Ava, I think we've said all we need to say. I'm tired of getting whiplash from you. I deserve better. Now go away and leave me alone."

When she started to close the door, I shoved my foot across the threshold, stopping her. She sent me a look that made my belly clench nervously.

"I was wrong yelling at you last weekend, and putting so many requirements on you," I said earnestly. "I talked to Marcella, and I realize now that I was being way too rigid and controlling. If you just give me a second chance, I promise to do better."

"The thing is Ava, last time was your second chance, remember?" Kathy sounded tired. "Now go away, please. And don't come over here again."

I left the flowers on the floor in front of her door and headed home, feeling dejected.

"So, you're just gonna give up that easily?" Marcella asked me an hour later.

I'd called her in tears, asking her to meet me for a drink. And good friend that she was, she'd blown off her date and headed right over to a dive bar near my house that we both really liked.

"What else can I do?" I asked, knocking back a shot of tequila.

"How did she look when you saw her?"

"What do you mean?" I asked. "Like what was she wearing?"

Marcella rolled her eyes. "No, when she told you to go away, did she look like she was about to cut you and then file a restraining order? Or did she look sad and tired?"

"Definitely sad and tired," I said as I gestured to the server for another round of shots. "Although she might have just been writing."

"That means there might be hope that you can salvage this, assuming the way she looked had more to do with you than a book."

"What?" I asked. "How?"

My best friend looked up at the ceiling, the way she did when she was deep in thought. "A grand gesture?"

I shook my head. "Kathy would hate a grand gesture."

"In that case, you're going to need to use the Grand Canyon method."

"What are you talking about?" I asked in confusion.

"You know how the Grand Canyon was created by water dripping against rock, on and on for hundreds of years, never letting up?"

"Yeah."

"You need to be the water, Ava."

"Are you drunk?" I asked her.

"Maybe a little, but my point is valid. You need to wear her down until one of two things happens."

"What two things?"

"Either she'll relent and give you another chance, or she'll get a restraining order. Either way, you'll know how to proceed."

CHAPTER THIRTY-FIVE – A GLIMMER OF HOPE

"Still no word from Kathy?" Marcella asked.

"No," I sighed. "It's been a month. I guess I need to take the hint and give up."

I'd spent the last four weeks trying to get back in Kathy's good graces. I sent her a little something every day. Her favorite ice cream. A card with a handwritten apology. A teddy bear holding a little sign that read 'You're my kind of girl.' Meals. And yesterday, a 'singing telegram' of the ten things I promised to do differently if she gave me another chance.

I was even desperate enough to get my mother involved. She'd stalked the coffee shop Kathy liked to frequent, waiting for her to come in. Unfortunately, Mom never saw her.

The biggest thing I'd done was more for myself than Kathy. I'd started seeing a counselor. I went into counseling thinking she'd help me deal with my emotions about losing Kathy but soon I realized that I had a lot of unresolved emotions from my last big break-up that had impacted my ability to be my whole self with Katy..

Mia was the reason that until I fell in love with Kathy I swore up and down I didn't want a relationship. She and I met at my job. She was a consultant my parents hired for a special project and right from the beginning there were sparks between us. We flirted around each other for two months until she was no longer working for us, then we'd started a relationship that burned hot and intense.

I thought I was in love with her, and I guess I was, but unfortunately Mia didn't feel the same. Oh, she said she loved me, but then she cheated on me. Repeatedly. She went away on a lot of business trips, which is likely why Kathy's disappearing acts bothered me so much, and while I was mooning around missing her, she was seeing other women. Something I only realized when I decided to surprise her and join her on a trip to Denver.

But she wasn't the one who was surprised. When I knocked on the door to her hotel room, another woman answered, wearing just a shirt and panties. Through the doorway I could see Mia on the bed in a similar state of undress. I didn't have to be a genius to figure out what was happening.

I hadn't dated anyone seriously since then. Until Kathy.

I thought I'd put all that behind me, but now that I was seeing a therapist, it was painfully obvious how the fallout from that relationship had affected my relationship with Kathy. Not that this was all on me, but I could at least see my part now.

Something I'd love to tell Kathy if she would just talk to me.

"It might be time to move on," Marcella said gently. "It's her loss though."

"It's both of our loss."

As I walked home from having drinks with Marcella I was so lost in thought that at first I didn't notice the figure sitting outside my door.

"Kathy." I blinked, trying to make sure I wasn't hallucinating.

She came to her feet and shoved a box at me. I could see the teddy bear on top, still holding the sign that read, *'You're my kind of girl'.*

"Stop sending me stuff!"

When she made to walk around me and leave I blurted out, "I'm in therapy."

She stopped but didn't turn around. "What?"

"I started going to therapy so I could see all the things I did wrong in our relationship and try to learn to be better."

She sighed deeply and turned to face me. "It wasn't just you. I'm crap at relationships too."

"Maybe we can both get better at it. Together."

She heaved another long sigh, but I could see that she was wavering.

"How about we talk?" I asked. "Just talk. And then if you don't want to see me again, I promise to leave you alone."

"Talk?" she confirmed.

I nodded. "Talk."

When she didn't move I reached out my hand. "Come inside."

CHAPTER THIRTY-SIX — A HAPPY ENDING

Kathy sat across from me at the kitchen table, nursing a beer while I gathered up my thoughts.

"I know I've been hot and cold with you," I started. "Well, cold and hot and cold and hot with a side of controlling, but I've done a lot of self-reflection while we've been apart, and my therapist has helped me to see that I'm treating you like I expect you to turn into Mia."

"Who's Mia?"

"She's an ex, my last serious girlfriend. She was a serial cheater," I explained. "She was away a lot and used that to hide what she was doing. So when I started dating you, and there were these periods of time where we couldn't connect, well, some part of my brain started catastrophizing that it wasn't just your writing, it was something else."

"Look Ava, I get that my communication skills aren't that great, and I promise I'm working on that, but we've tried being together and it's not worked out. Maybe we just need to cut our losses. It shouldn't be this hard."

"I have a proposal. Let's go to couple's counseling."

She looked surprised. "Couples counseling? If we need that kind of help now, I really don't think this is going to work out long term."

"A neutral third party can help us with our communication skills and help us learn to move past what's happened before, so we don't keep hurting each other."

She shook her head. "I don't know."

"Let me ask you a question. Do you love me?"

She was quiet so long I thought she wasn't going to answer. Finally she said, "I do love you, Ava. But sometimes love isn't enough."

"This isn't a romance book, Kathy. Real relationships are hard. They take work," I said. "In real life there's a lot of things that happen between the meet cute and the happily ever after and it's not all sunshine and rainbows. But I love you and you love me, and one thing that I know for sure is that my life is way worse without you in it. "

I moved around the table to kneel by her chair, taking both of her hands in mine. "I miss you, Kathy."

Her eyes looked a little shiny. "I miss you too."

"How about this? Instead of a second or a third chance, how about we have a new beginning? We'll do things right this time."

I pushed to my feet and stuck out my hand. "Hello, my name is Ava Morganstein. And my mother, who loves me very much, is absolutely certain that we'd be a good couple."

She stared at my hand for a second before taking it. "Hi, I'm Kathy Olsen. It's nice to meet you Ava."

I gave her a slow smile. "Kathy, I don't mean to be forward, but I have to tell you that you are one of the most beautiful women I've seen in my life."

A slight blush rose up Kathy's face.

"If you're free tonight, I'd love to take you to dinner," I continued. "There's a great Italian restaurant up the street that makes the most incredible spinach lasagna."

"I love spinach lasagna," Kathy responded, still playing the game. In reality, we'd gone to that restaurant half a dozen times.

"How about we walk down to the restaurant, I'll buy you some lasagna, and we can get to know each other?"

She paused, and for a minute I thought maybe she'd pull back again, but instead she gave me a big smile.

"I think I'd like that, Ava. But there is something you should know about me."

"What?"

"I want a happily ever after, but I'm not willing to settle to get it."

I squeezed the hand that I was still holding. "Don't worry, you'll never have to settle with me. I'll treat you like a queen."

Kathy gave me a tremulous smile. "I'll settle for you treating me like an equal."

"That I can do. Now how about we get that lasagna?"

CHAPTER THIRTY-SEVEN – EPILOGUE: A BUNDLE OF JOY

*T*hree years later...

"Are you sure you want to do this?" Kathy looked a little green around the gills.

I patted the overstretched skin on my stomach, ignoring the slight pressure I was feeling from the baby moving downward.

"It's a little too late to change our minds now," I teased. "Don't worry. The doctor said this has been a textbook pregnancy. I'm going to be fine, and the baby is going to be fine."

I paused to grip her forearm as another contraction hit. We'd already been to the hospital once and sent home because it wasn't quite time. But now the contractions were four minutes apart and as soon as my father arrived with his car, we were heading back to the hospital. Thanks to so many years living in the big city, Kathy had never learned to drive.

"You'd better both be fine," Kathy said sternly. "I won't allow any other result."

I gave her a smile. Even after all this time together, I was still always a little surprised when my seemingly mild-mannered wife let out her alpha side. That stern voice got me every time. But there was no time for any funny business. Our baby was ready to finally make his or her appearance.

After our fresh start Kathy and I started going to couple's counseling. Three months in, our therapist deemed that we were in a good place to stop, but we made the occasional appointment whenever something big was happening. We did a couple of sessions before we moved in together, another one before we got married, and at least three when we decided to get pregnant.

Neither of us doubted that we wanted a baby, we just weren't sure if it was the right time, and we had a hard time deciding who would be the one to get inseminated. In the end, we decided I would take the first one, and Kathy would carry our second. One thing we both agreed on was that two kids would be the perfect number for us.

We got married last year. Despite my mother's protestations to the contrary, we'd insisted on a very small and intimate ceremony, with just close friends and family present. It was perfect for us. We'd splurged on a honeymoon in Paris and had enjoyed every minute of our six days wandering around the City of Love.

In preparation for our expanded family, Kathy sold her townhouse, and I tapped my trust fund so we could buy a larger place that was just ours. We'd moved to Skokie, a close-in suburb that had a reputation for being liberal and had good schools. Both of us were bemused that good schools were now one of our factors for choosing a location. Apparently we were grown-ups now.

My father pulled up just as another contraction hit, my mother in the front seat. Dad and Kathy maneuvered me into the backseat and Dad floored the gas pedal.

"Dad! I've got time. Be careful," I admonished.

Several hours later the doctor put a beautiful baby girl into my arms. We'd chosen to be surprised, so we had no idea that we'd get a girl, but it felt perfect that we had. Little Amelia, as we'd named her, was already showing her personality, her face turning red as she shrieked in outrage that I was taking too long to latch her onto a nipple.

"Aw, she looks just like her Mama when she has a temper tantrum," Kathy teased.

She stroked Amelia's leg, and the baby calmed down as soon as she got access to food. While I nursed, Kathy slipped up on the bed next to us, one arm going around my shoulder, the other still stroking the baby's leg.

"I love you," she whispered as she pressed a kiss to my temple. "What you just did was so brave. You were so strong. I have never loved you more."

I gave her a wry look. "Now that you've seen childbirth you want me to carry the next one too, don't you?"

She had the good grace to look guilty. "Did I mention that I love you?"

***

If you liked this book, please consider leaving a review or rating to let me know. Keep reading for a special preview of Reba Bale's lesbian romance "The Divorcee's First Time".

You can find more of Reba's lesbian romances at Bo oks2read.com/rl/lesbianromance

Be sure to join my newsletter for more great books. You'll receive a free lesbian romance book when you sign up. Subscribers are the first to hear about all of my new releases and sales. Visit my mailing list sign-up at https://books.r ebabale.com/lesbianromance to download your free book today.

Special Preview of The Divorcee's First Time

A Contemporary Lesbian Romance by Reba Bale

"It's done," I said triumphantly. "My divorce is final."

My best friend Susan paused in the process of sliding into the restaurant booth, her sharply manicured eyebrows raising almost to her hairline. "Dickhead finally signed the papers?" she asked, her tone hopeful.

I nodded as Susan settled into the seat across from me. "The judge signed off on it today. Apparently his barely legal girlfriend is knocked up, and she wants to get a ring on her finger before the big event." I explained with a touch of irony in my voice. "The child bride finally got it done for me."

Susan smiled and nodded. "Well congratulations and good riddance. Let's order some wine."

We were most of the way through our second bottle when the conversation turned back to my ex. "I wonder if Dickhead and his Child Bride will last for the long haul," Susan mused.

I shook my head and blew a chunk of hair away from my mouth.

"I doubt it," I told her. "Someday she's gonna roll over and think, there's got to be something better out there than a self-absorbed man child who doesn't know a clitoris from a doorknob."

Susan laughed, sputtering her wine. I eyed her across the table. Although she was ten years older than me, we had been best friends for the last five years. We worked together at the accounting firm. She had been my trainer when I first came there, fresh out of school with my degree. We bonded over work, but soon realized that we were kindred spirits.

Susan was rapidly approaching forty but could easily pass for my age. Her hair was black and shiny, hinting at her Puerto Rican heritage, with blunt bangs and blond highlights that she paid a fortune for. Her face was clear and unlined, with large brown eyes and cheek bones that could cut glass. She was an avid runner and worked hard to maintain a slim physique since the women in her family ran towards the chunkier side.

I was almost her complete opposite. Blonde curls to her straight dark hair, blue eyes instead of brown, curvy where she was lean, introverted to her extrovert.

But somehow, we clicked. We were closer than sisters. Honestly, I don't know how I would have gotten through the last year without her. She had been the first one I called when my marriage fell apart, and she had supported me throughout the whole process.

It had been a big shock when I came home early one day and found my husband getting a blow job in the middle of our living room. It had been even more shocking when I saw the fresh young face at the other end of that blow job.

"What the fuck are you doing?" I had screeched, startling them both out of their sex stupor. "You're getting blow jobs from children now?"

The girl had looked up from her knees with eyes glowing in righteous indignation. "I'm not a child, I'm nineteen," she had informed me proudly. "I'm glad you finally found out. I give him what you don't, and he loves me."

I looked into the familiar eyes of my husband and saw the panic and confusion there. I made it easy for him. "Get out," I told him firmly, my voice leaving no room for argument. "Take your teenage girlfriend and get the fuck out. We're getting a divorce. Expect to hear from my lawyer."

The condo was in my name. I had purchased it before we were married, and since I had never added his name to the deed, he had no rights to it. There was no question he would be the one leaving.

My husband just stared at me with his jaw hanging open like he couldn't believe it. "But Jennifer," he whined. "You don't understand. Let me explain."

"There's nothing to understand," I told him sadly. "This is a deal breaker for me, and you know that as well as I do. We are done."

The girl had taken his hand and smiled triumphantly. "Come on baby," she told him. "Zip up and let's get out of here. We can finally be together like we planned."

"Yeah baby," I had sneered. "I'll box up your stuff. It'll be in the hallway tomorrow. Pick it up by six o'clock or I'm trashing it all."

After they left my first call was to the locksmith, but my second call was to Susan.

That night was the last time I had seen my husband until we had met for the court-ordered pre-divorce mediation. He spent most of that session reiterating what he had told me in numerous voice mails, emails and sessions spent yelling on the other side of my front door. He loved me. He had made a terrible mistake. He wasn't going to sign the papers. We were meant to be together. Needless to say, mediation hadn't been very successful. Fortunately, I had been careful to keep our assets separate, as if I knew that someday I would be in this situation.

Through it all, Susan had been my rock. In the end I don't think I was even that sad about the divorce, I was really angrier with myself for staying in a relationship that wasn't fulfilling with a man I didn't love anymore.

"You need to get some quality sex." Susan drew my attention back to the present. "Bang him out of your system."

"I don't know," I answered slowly. "I think I need a hiatus."

"A hiatus from what?" Susan asked with a frown. "You haven't had sex in what, eighteen months?"

I nodded. "Yeah, but I just can't take a disappointing fumble right now. I would rather have nothing than another three-pump chump."

I shook my head and continued, "I'm going to stick with my battery-operated boyfriend, he never disappoints me."

Susan smiled. "That's because you know your way around your own vajayjay."

She motioned to the waiter to bring us a third bottle of wine.

"That's why I like to date women," she continued. "We already know our way around the equipment."

I nodded thoughtfully. "You make a good point."

Susan leaned forward. "We've never talked about this," she said earnestly. "Have you ever been with a woman?"

For more of the story, check out "The Divorcee's First Time" by Reba Bale, available for immediate download at https://books2read.com/Divorcee.

***

Want a free book? Join my newsletter and a special gift. I'll contact you a few times a month with story updates, new releases, and special sales. Visit bit.ly/RebaBaleSapphic for more information.

OTHER BOOKS BY REBA BALE

Check out my other books, available on most major online retailers now. Go to at bit.ly/AuthorRebaBale to learn more.

Friends to Lovers Lesbian Romance Series

The Divorcee's First Time

My BFF's Sister

My Rockstar Assistant

My College Crush

My Fake Girlfriend

My Secret Crush

My Holiday Love

My Valentine's Gift

My Spring Fling

My Forbidden Love

My Office Wife

My Second Chance

Coming Out in Ten Dates

Worth Waiting For

My Party Planner

My Broken Heart

My New Teacher

The Surrender Club Lesbian Romance Series

Jaded

Hated

Fated

Saved

Caged

Dared

The Sapphic Security Series

Guarding the Senator's Daughter

Guarding the Rock Star

Guarding the Witness

Guarding the Billionaire

Playing to Win Lesbian Sports Series

Tumbling for Love

Racing for Love

Spiking for Love

The Second Chances Lesbian Romance Series

Last Christmas

The Summer I Fell in Love

Snowed in With You

My Kind of Girl

Menage Romances

Pie Promises

Tornado Warning

Summer in Paradise

Life of the Mardi

Bases Loaded

Two for One Deal

Penalty Box

Rock My Heart

The Unexpectedly Mine Series

Sinful Desires

Taken by Surprise

Just One Night

Forbidden Desires

Spanking & Sprinkles

Hotwife Erotic Romances

Hotwife in the Woods

Hotwife on the Beach

Hotwife Under the Tree

A Hotwife's Retreat

Hot Wife Happy Life

Want a free book? Just join my newsletter at https:// books.rebabale.com/lesbian. You'll be the first to hear about new releases, special sales, and free offers.

ABOUT REBA BALE

Reba Bale writes erotic romance, lesbian romance, menage romance, & the spicy stories you want to read on a cold winter's night.

She lives in the Northwest with her family and two very spoiled dogs. When Reba is not writing she is reading the same naughty stories she likes to write.

For all of Reba's stories visit her webpage at https://books2read.com/rebabale.

You can also follow Reba on Ream and Medium for free stories, bonus epilogues and more. You can hear all about new releases and special sales by joining Reba's mailing list at *https://books.rebabale.com/lesbianromance*

Printed in Dunstable, United Kingdom

71710587R00121